PRAISE FOR EMMA SHEVAH'S BOOKS

*'By turns playful and poignant, in both style and substance,
this coming-of-age novel will hook readers
from the first page to the last.'*
SCHOOL LIBRARY JOURNAL, STARRED REVIEW

'. . . a beautifully written story.'
INDEPENDENT ON SUNDAY

'Funny, poignant . . . [a] wise and accessible read.'
WALL STREET JOURNAL

'Amber's oddball voice makes the lessons go down easy.'
NEW YORK TIMES

*'A funny and heart-warming novel about modern-day
families, starting school, being of mixed race
and celebrating your uniqueness.'*
LOVEREADING4KIDS

*'. . . snappily narrated and exuberantly illustrated,
[Dara Palmer's Major Drama] is sure to win readers over.'*
PUBLISHERS WEEKLY

*'. . . a wonderfully modern voice that manages to perfectly
balance a sensitive subject with light and laughter.'*
BOOKTRUST

'Fun and thought-provoking.'
PEOPLE MAGAZINE

A message from Chicken House

There are lots of funny names for them – porky-pies, whoppers, fibs – but lies aren't funny at all. Really, they aren't! Emma Shevah shows a family torn apart by Lexie's untruth. You will find yourself shouting out loud at them all – because everything can be saved by a simple truth, but who is brave enough to own up? Funny and heart-wrenching, this is a fantastic book for anyone who has ever been tempted to tell a big fat lie!

BARRY Cunningham
Publisher

WHAT LEXIE DID

Emma Shevah

Illustrations by *Helen Crawford-White*

Chicken House

2 Palmer Street, Frome, Somerset BA11 1DS
www.chickenhousebooks.com

Text © Emma Shevah 2018

First published in Great Britain in 2018
Chicken House
2 Palmer Street
Frome, Somerset BA11 1DS
United Kingdom
www.chickenhousebooks.com

Cover, illustration and interior design by Helen Crawford-White
Printed and bound in Great Britain by CPI Group (UK) Ltd, Croydon CR0 4YY

The paper used in this Chicken House book is made
from wood grown in sustainable forests.

1 3 5 7 9 10 8 6 4 2

British Library Cataloguing in Publication data available.

PB ISBN 978-1-910655-46-7
eISBN 978-1-911077-49-7

To Sean, my cousin and almost-twin. Born
two weeks after me and pushed around
in the same pram, we grew up sharing
games, jokes and birthday parties, and
years later, we had our children a
few months apart. You are my Eleni.

Also by Emma Shevah

Dream On, Amber
Dara Palmer's Major Drama

PART

1

1

Have you ever been so close to someone that you could wah-wah in whale song?

I have. Well, sort of, anyway.

When I say 'wah-wah', I mean communicate, but not in a normal way. In a special telepathic way that wah-wahs out of your brain and into theirs, or wah-wahs out of their brain into yours. Come to think of it, it's nothing like whale song. I don't know why we ever thought it was, but when we were little that's what Eleni called it, and it stuck. Look, we were about five at the time, and when you're five, the craziest nonsense makes perfect sense.

What our five-year-old brains were trying to say was this: sometimes two human beings know each other so well, they can talk in a language that isn't made up of

words. It isn't made up of eye squints, hand twists or face gymnastics, either. No. This communication is much more wooOOohhh and spooky than that (just without the aliens and ghosts).

You can only wah-wah with someone you're super-crazy-mega-extra-*seriously* close to, and for me, that person is Eleni.

She's my cousin, but the word 'cousin' needs an update, if you ask me. You know how some languages have tons of words to describe one thing? I looked up 'Eskimo words for snow' once, and found out that the Sami people of Scandinavia and Russia use around 180 snow-and-ice-related words, and 300 words for types of snow, snow conditions and snow tracks. Even more mind-blowing, they use around a thousand words for reindeer.

A thousand words!
FOR *REINDEER*!

I was so amazed by that, I had to write some down in my notebook.

Sami words for specific types of reindeer:

- short fat female
- pregnant female
- female that has not given birth to a calf that year
- female that lost her calf in late spring
- female that can never have a calf
- miserable, skinny female without a proper coat
- miserable, skinny male without a proper coat
- young healthy male advanced enough to accompany his mother in difficult conditions
- dark yellowish-grey male with brown belly
- males with no antlers/cut antlers/many-branched antlers/tall, quivering antlers (etc.)
- lazy old hand-biters
- flying red-nosed present-deliverers

(I might have made those last two up.)

Cyprus

Guitar

So it's strange that there's only one word for cousin. Cousins aren't all the same – there are *degrees* of cousin-ness. Some are close as twins, like Eleni and me, and some are people you barely know. Amy Mitchell in my class has cousins she's only met once because they live in Germany.

Weird.

The only person I know who has more first cousins than us is Mohammed Rashid. We have twenty-eight and he has forty or fifty – he doesn't know the exact number – but his are spread all over the world and ours all live in the same five-mile radius of South London. I bet if we could, we'd all live in the same house. Maybe even the same *room*.

When I grow up, I'm going to write dictionaries and invent a thousand words for 'cousin'. These are just a few of the very complicated rankings:

Degrees of cousin-ness:

Categories:

• Cousin on mum or dad's side

- Older or younger than you
- Degree of hairiness

Sub-categories:
- How close they live to you
- How often you see them
- How well you get on
- How many games you make up together
- How likely you are to win

Like-ability:
- Do they fire Nerf guns at you/stick jelly sweets in your shoes/give good birthday presents/let you watch stuff you're not allowed to watch when they're babysitting at your house?
- Are they a bit strange but you need to be nice to them or you'll get shouted at?
- Are they useful to know later, like Vasillis, who's a locksmith?

As for Eleni, she's the closest a cousin could possibly be. Closer than *anyone* could be. I mean, if it's possible to have a twin who isn't *really* your twin – like not from the same egg or mother, but a twin deep down in your heart and your cells and your soul, or something – then Eleni is mine.

We don't look like twins. My hair's dark brown, but it looks a little reddish in the sun. It's also thick and wavy, and even though Mum makes me tie it up, it still gushes to my waist in a hair waterfall. Eleni's hair is light brown, and it's so fine and straight and thin, it's more like a hair dribbly tap. She has a small, pointy nose and huge hazel-green eyes, so if you ask me, she looks a bit like a bushbaby. My eyes are chocolate-brown, I've just got new glasses and I look more like a human being. I'm strong and fit but Eleni's weak and as skinny as a sweeping brush because of her complication. That's one of the reasons we're so close, but I'll come to that later.

So we might not look identical, but that doesn't mean anything. We're twins anyway. And we need each other for all kinds of things. Eleni's terrified of the dark and of spiders, and she freaks at fireworks, thunder and the sound of bath water being sucked down the plughole. She makes me go into rooms and turn lights on, do spider checks under the beds and unplug the bath for her so she can run away to a safe place with her hands over her ears, yelling.

And when I worry too much about the bad things in the world, she reminds me of some of the good things, like pizza with pineapple, snowy days and watching cartoons in pyjamas, to make me feel better. We have notebooks full of them, just in case, and write lists of them all the time so we have them whenever we need them.

So I make sure the bath monster doesn't suck Eleni down the plughole and she reminds me that because the world contains conkers, hummingbirds and chocolate brownies, everything is going to be just fine.

What I'm trying to say is that we look out for each other. We always have. And we always will. Least that's what I thought. But then something bad happened, which led to some *really* bad stuff happening, and then I did something that changed everything.

After that, we forgot we were basically twins, and that we were once so close we could wah-wah in whale song.

And it all started with the picnic.

9

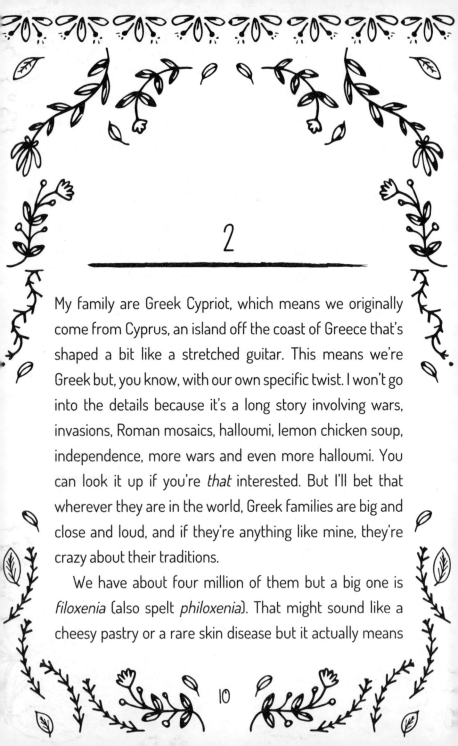

2

My family are Greek Cypriot, which means we originally come from Cyprus, an island off the coast of Greece that's shaped a bit like a stretched guitar. This means we're Greek but, you know, with our own specific twist. I won't go into the details because it's a long story involving wars, invasions, Roman mosaics, halloumi, lemon chicken soup, independence, more wars and even more halloumi. You can look it up if you're *that* interested. But I'll bet that wherever they are in the world, Greek families are big and close and loud, and if they're anything like mine, they're crazy about their traditions.

We have about four million of them but a big one is *filoxenia* (also spelt *philoxenia*). That might sound like a cheesy pastry or a rare skin disease but it actually means 'friend to foreigners'. It comes from the Greek myth about Zeus, king of the gods, when he disguised himself as a poor man in rags and visited the homes of Greeks to see how they treated strangers.

'So-u,' Yiayia, my grandma, says. (Don't ask me why but she pronounces it like it has a 'u' on the end. Greeks also drag words out so they're really long, and the sounds and rhythms go up and down like a melody.) 'You must always treat the strangers very very good, Alexandra, because maybe they turn out to be the *god*.'

Yiayia's the only one who still calls me Alexandra. Like me, most Greeks are named after saints, but we usually give each other nicknames or our names get shortened. I got called Alexia, then Lexie, and half the time they even shorten *that* to Lex.

Anyhow, *filoxenia* is the reason we had the picnic near Brighton that Saturday: we wanted to welcome the new family and have an excuse – not that we ever need one – to eat ten tons of Greek food. The Antoniou family weren't exactly strangers. We're not talking about mysterious visitors from a distant land or anything. They were Greek Cypriots who'd moved from North to South London.

The dad was Mum's friend's cousin, and the mum was someone's sister-in-law, but they were new in our neighbourhood, and that was enough.

So we had one of those big family-and-friends picnics where the adults talk extra-loudly, the teenagers gang together and act bored, and the little kids chase each other with dog poo on sticks. We have them a couple of times a year anyhow, and there's always a serious amount of food. Mainly meat for the barbeque, but also salads, fruit, and lemon cake. And even though there are normally about forty or fifty Greek people there, we always bring enough food for fifty more.

As for all that Zeus stuff, well . . . let me put it like this: their daughter did not turn out to be a god in disguise. Uh-uh. Right from the start I didn't like her. I don't know why. I usually like everyone, but there was something about her that made my skin prickle and my eyes squeeze into slits. It might have been because she kept trying to take my best friend and almost-twin away from me, but there was more to it than that. She got on my nerves and that's just the way it was.

Her name was Anastasia and I liked her as much as I

liked eating slugs and wearing itchy knickers. Still, when she threw our car keys in the sea, she taught me a big life lesson. It wasn't that you don't throw car keys in the sea. I knew that already. I don't know why she didn't, because you'd think it was pretty obvious.

No. What she taught me that day is that sometimes in life you have to lie.

You do. Honest.

And when I say this was a 'big life lesson', I'm not exaggerating either, but we'll get to that part later, too.

Even though it was September, it was still warm and sunny. Eleni and I found a good spot near the dunes, spread out a prickly blanket and pulled off our socks. Then we breathed in the salty seaweed air and listened to the screechy gulls and the foamy hiss of the waves. That's pretty much heaven to me: being outdoors on a sunny day with Eleni, our notebooks at our knees. On the downside, I'm not that into prickly blankets but you can't have heaven outside of real heaven or real heaven wouldn't be a thing (if you know what I mean).

First, we named the dogs running around on the beach (Gungadin, Slobberchops and Felicity Whipple). Then we

thought up ways of describing the sky and the sea and wrote them in our notebooks. It was a hazy lazy pick-a-daisy kind of day and the clouds looked like huge frothy thoughts puffing up and out of a giant's brain, so I wrote that down in mine. Eleni said the stones on the beach were magical brown and grey eggs laid by Great Mother Ocean, and that the air felt warm but not hot, like a five-minute-old cup of hot chocolate, so she wrote that down in hers.

Insects buzzed busily about. Wasps zoomed in for my apple juice. *Where do they go all winter?* I wondered. I'd just turned to ask Eleni when I saw Anastasia walking over holding a colourful stick with a hoop at the end.

She was taller than us and wore a bright green sparkly dress with dark green Dr Marten boots. She had thick curls tied up high on her head, large brown eyes with extra-long lashes and a gap between her front teeth. Eleni thought she was cool and funky – those were her exact words when Anastasia stepped out of the car in that electric-leprechaun outfit. Personally, I thought she was annoying and unwelcome – a bit like a wasp at a picnic, funnily enough.

14

Anastasia shoved our notebooks on to the stones and sat on our rug. I scowled at our treasured notebooks lying in a heap. Sorry, but you don't push people's precious things away like that. You just don't.

'Picnics are *lit*erally lame,' she said, rolling her eyes. She didn't seem to care that we'd all come out that day to welcome her and her family OR that she was using 'literally' in the wrong way. How can a picnic be *literally* lame? It doesn't even have legs.

Eleni grinned. 'Picnic food is always in a hurry,' she said. 'You know why?'

A cheesy joke was coming. I could just tell.

'Because it's fast food!' She started laughing her head off, but neither of us got it. I was frowning at her and so was Anastasia.

'You know! Fast food? It's travelled really fast on the motorway?' Eleni said. And then she cracked up again.

Anastasia burst out laughing, even though it was clearly only a two-out-of-ten joke. Maybe even one out of ten. 'I've heard about you,' she said to Eleni. 'You're the miracle girl. No one told me you were so funny, though. Hahahaha-haha.'

Eleni beamed. I bit the skin on the inside of my cheek and smiled weakly.

'Want a go?' Anastasia held up her skipping hopper. I wasn't sure who she was talking to, but she wasn't looking at me. I didn't answer her at first, but ohhh, I wanted a go. Badly. But Eleni couldn't run or jump much so I wasn't going to say yes and leave her sitting there. Anyhow, I didn't want anything to do with someone who shoved our notebooks away and called our family picnics 'literally lame'. Eleni wouldn't either. I mean, *seriously?*

'No, thanks. Don't like those things,' I lied.

'I do!' Eleni hollered. When I whipped my head around to frown at her, she added, 'I'll be fine,' and shot up with a giggle.

'We're going to be best friends, I can just tell,' Anastasia said with a huge grin as they walked a few metres away to a flatter part of the beach. The salty clean air in my lungs turned into a dark, swirling smog. Anastasia put the hoop around Eleni's ankle and she started spinning the stick and jumping over it, laughing. Steam hissed out of my head but I picked up my sparkly notebook like it didn't bother me.

'Cooooooome,' Eleni called in whale song.

'Noooooooo,' I replied, pouting.

Instead, I squinted at my notebook with my brain boiling. Why had I lied like that? I never usually lied. I didn't like the way it made me feel, but also, adults always made out as if the truth was something pure and holy, and maybe they were right. The word 'truth' even *sounded* holy. *Truuuttth, Lexie. Trrrrruuuuuuuttttthhhhhh.* I could hear it calling me, like angels singing 'ahhhhh' over the surface of the sea but in really deep voices.

The truth was, I desperately wanted a go on that stupid hoppy thing and now I was sitting alone with wasps buzzing by my ear, feeling sad and grumpy.

This, I told myself, *this is what happens when you lie, Lexie. Telling the truth would have made you happy. And now look at you.* It was as if a mini angel with a voice like a headmistress was standing on my earlobe and shouting into my ear. But she had a point. At that moment, the truth about the truth smacked me in the face (in a pure, angelic way).

Lying wasn't only bad because the truth was holy – it was bad because lying made you unhappy.

HUH!

Why hadn't I realized that before?

That was it, I decided. From now on, I was going to tell the truth. Next time and every time.

Even if it meant saying yes to someone as grrr as Anastasia.

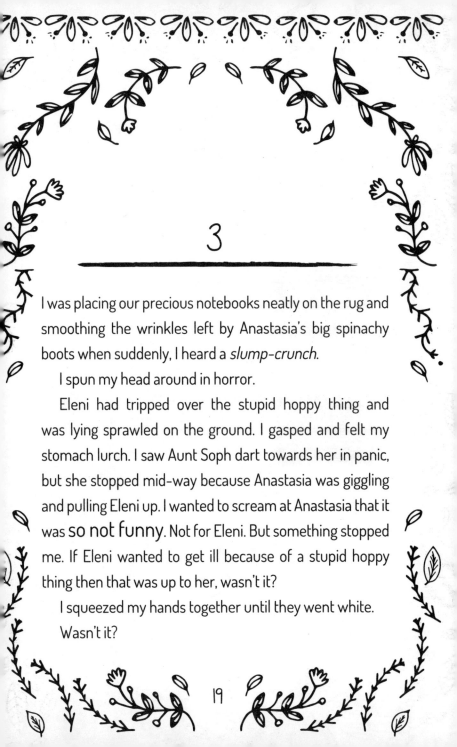

3

I was placing our precious notebooks neatly on the rug and smoothing the wrinkles left by Anastasia's big spinachy boots when suddenly, I heard a *slump-crunch*.

I spun my head around in horror.

Eleni had tripped over the stupid hoppy thing and was lying sprawled on the ground. I gasped and felt my stomach lurch. I saw Aunt Soph dart towards her in panic, but she stopped mid-way because Anastasia was giggling and pulling Eleni up. I wanted to scream at Anastasia that it was so not funny. Not for Eleni. But something stopped me. If Eleni wanted to get ill because of a stupid hoppy thing then that was up to her, wasn't it?

I squeezed my hands together until they went white. Wasn't it?

What if it wasn't?

I watched in case I had to run over and help her. A cloud lingered overhead and the sky went a dull dark grey, or maybe that was just me.

Once she got her breath back, Eleni stumbled towards me and flopped on the rug, panting. 'Should . . . have come. So . . . much . . . fun.'

'You OK?'

'Yep,' she said, wheezing. 'That . . . hopper . . . is so cool . . . How nice is she? I . . . totally . . . love her.'

'Mmm.' I glared at Anastasia. She was jogging over to where Nicos (my brother) and Elias (Eleni's brother) were playing football, and the other kids were playing 'Truth or Dare': I could tell because my cousin Kallie always dares people to walk in the sea with their shoes on, and my sister Kat was at the edge, about to wade in. I saw Kallie whisper in Anastasia's ear, which was bad news. I wondered what dumb dare it was going to be this time.

I didn't have to wait long to find out. Eleni was still lying on the rug, panting, when Anastasia dashed over to one of the picnic tables, grabbed something and ran towards the sea. After the dash was a flash, then a gasp from the other

20

kids, who scattered in all directions.

Eleni sat up and asked, 'What *was* that?'

I shook my head. *That can't have just happened. It can't have.*

I was still digesting it when, two minutes later, Dad started roaring in his megaphone voice, 'For crying out loud! Where are the car keys?'

My eyes whooshed wide, like I was having goldfish lessons. Dad was not going to like the answer to that question. Not one little bit.

Oh, I knew where they were, all right. I'd seen Anastasia grab them off the picnic table and hurl them backwards over her head. I'd heard them fall with a *dip-plop* and watched round ripples wrinkle the surface of the water. And I'd seen Anastasia clap her hands over her mouth and bomb it down the beach. But it happened so quickly. The adults had been doing a million other things: fussing over foil, rustling packets and making snapped-box sounds.

'Andy!' Mum screeched, like it was his fault. 'The *koubes* are in the car!' She was desperate to show them off after all her hard work making them.

'Yeah, that's right, Ange,' Dad bellowed, 'panic about the

21

food. Who cares if we can't get home tonight? The *koubes* are stuck in the car!'

Uncle Christos burst out laughing.

'I'm not *panicking*!' Mum shouted. She was totally panicking. She's very dramatic, my mother. If she was on the stage she'd be accused of overacting, but that's how she is in real life.

I sat there, paralysed, thinking, *oh em gee. Should I tell them?*

'Check your pockets!' Mum yelled at Dad. 'What about the cooler bag?'

'They were **right there**!' Dad said, pointing at the picnic table.

I watched, feeling more and more sick.

'You OK, Lex?' Eleni asked. 'You've gone a bit white.'

I had to tell them the truth. I had to. The truth was high and holy, and hummed with luminous light, a bit like a nun version of Tinkerbell. And telling the truth would make me happy, too. It would make everyone happy.

Hadn't I just learnt that?

4

I ran to where my dad was digging in the sand, tapped his shoulder and pointed at the sea. It took my dad a second to figure it out. My finger. The sea. My finger. The sea. What did that have to do with—?

And then his eyes shrieked *NO!* And my eyes replied, *YES!* (I'm good at eye conversations as well as whale ones.)

'Wait. What are you saying, Lex?' Dad asked, using words this time. (He clearly wasn't as good at eye conversations as I thought.) 'Don't tell me the keys in the sea.'

Well, that was confusing. Did he want the truth or didn't he? I paused for a second, trying to work it out.

'Lexie. Tell me the truth,' he added. Which was good timing, I can tell you.

So I spelt it out in actual words from my actual mouth.

'The keys are in the sea, Dad.'

'Jesus Christ!' he shouted, but I don't think he said it in a holy way. Then he asked, 'Why, Lexie? Why are the keys in the sea?'

That seemed obvious to me, but I had to tell him anyway – he wasn't that good at working things out for himself, I'd just realized. So I said slowly, 'Because some-one threw them in there, Dad.'

'*WHAT?* Which idiot's done that?' Dad yelled.

I knew exactly which idiot had done it but I wasn't going to go to heaven if I told on Anastasia, was I? Mind you, I wasn't going to heaven if I lied to my dad's face, either.

When adults ask you so bluntly, what are you supposed to say?

'Tell me the truth and you won't get into trouble,' Dad said. 'No one will.' He leant so close, the dark caves of his nostrils looked like they were going to swallow me up. I had to look away before he ate me with his face.

He put his hot heavy hand on my shoulder. He was guiding me towards the truth, and it felt safe. As if to prove it, the angels began to sing *ah-ahhhhh* in the air above my head (or maybe just inside my head). 'Who did it, Lexie?'

So I said, 'Anastasia.' Because no one would get in trouble if I told the truth. Wasn't that what Dad said? Isn't that what all adults say?

Yeah, right.

You should have seen them. Everyone started shouting and throwing their arms around. Greeks have hand gestures for pretty much every situation, including *Andreas's keys are in the sea!* Surprisingly.

In the commotion, Nicos didn't save Elias's goal. Elias leapt up, screeched, 'YESSS!' and pulled his T-shirt up over his face, which wasn't a pleasant sight because he has a wobbly belly and man boobs. Kat and Kallie were hiding behind a car by then, but I could see them glaring at me like they wanted to chuck *me* in the sea as well.

The adults waded in and fished for the keys in the exact spot I pointed to before the car keys got swept out to Spain or Morocco or whatever's south of Brighton.

Anastasia got in a juggernaut of trouble.

But – check this out – **so did I for telling on her!**

As Uncle C pulled the dripping keys out of the water with a roar of victory, and the adults clapped and cheered, the kids crowded around me to deliver their verdicts.

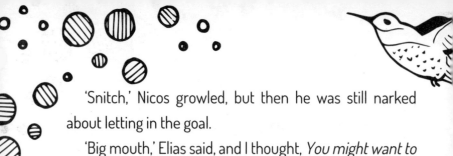

'Snitch,' Nicos growled, but then he was still narked about letting in the goal.

'Big mouth,' Elias said, and I thought, *You might want to close YOUR big mouth a little more, blubber belly.*

'Grass,' my sister snarled.

'Traitor.'

'Rat.'

Eleni stood by my side. She knows not to get involved in cousin wars, but she came to back me up because she always does. And she always will. No matter what.

Except that's not what happened.

When Anastasia came storming over to me and said, 'Can't believe what a tell-tale you are,' with eyes plotting the kind of revenge that wouldn't be sending *her* to heaven, Eleni did something odd. Instead of telling Anastasia to get lost or saying that throwing car keys in the sea was utterly brainless, she frowned at me and said, 'Lexie, what the heck? You got her in trouble.'

What? Why aren't you standing up for me? I asked Eleni in whale song. But she didn't answer.

'I just told the tru—' I began, but Anastasia's parents yelled, 'ANASTASIA! Get over here right now!' and she ran off.

I slumped on the itchy rug and gazed at the churning sea. By then, the sky was turning yellow, like a ghostly bowl of custard. Like the fragile fluttering wing of a lemon butterfly. Like a dome of omelette made from the yolks of a hundred homesick hens. I would have written it all in my notebook if I wasn't cringing right then with confusion and shame.

Maybe I **should have** told my dad where the keys were but said I **didn't know who did it.** Except that would have been lying, and lying made you unhappy.

But now the truth had made me unhappy too, and everyone else as well.

Eleni sat down next to me but I couldn't look at her. Three centuries went by in a minute or two.

'What should I have done?' I murmured eventually.

'Next time, lie,' Eleni said, matter-of-factly. She was feed-ing ants and seeing how much they could carry, which was quite a lot, and then she started counting them, even though they kept moving around and it was impossible. She loves counting things. She didn't seem to notice that she'd just blatantly betrayed me. 'I lie all the time,' she added.

27

I paused for a second to take that information in.

'You do?'

'Yep.'

I paused again. I couldn't tell if she was lying. That's the problem: once someone tells you that they lie, how do you know if you can believe them?

'Tell me one of your lies, then,' I said.

'I was tired after jumping with that hopper even though I said I was fine.'

'Knew it.'

She grinned and I glared at her. Something had just happened between us and I was still trying to figure it out. Meanwhile, maybe she was right. Maybe I did need to lie. But it felt so wrong! I didn't know if I could. I was a good girl. I helped at home, read books without being bribed and smiled in photos instead of sticking my tongue out. I looked after Eleni, sang the hymns in church and ate vegetables without smothering them in ketchup. I liked being good. But look where being good had got me.

'Fine. Next time I won't make that mistake,' I mumbled. 'Next time I'll do the right thing and lie.'

5

When we climbed in the car to go home, Nicos said, 'I'm not sitting next to *her*,' and took the seat behind Dad. Then Nicos put his headphones on and stared out of the window moodily, but that's what he does when he's happy as well, so it's nothing new. Kat sat in the middle, but she wouldn't let my leg touch hers: she kept shoving it away with her hand. If I ever had to create a villain for a story, I swear it would be a big sister. I sat behind Mum and imagined Kat and Nick's car seats eating them and that was fun for a while, but it still hurt.

After a few minutes, Mum turned to Kat and Nick and pointed a finger in the air. 'Be nice to your sister, you two. Enough of the cold-shoulder stuff.'

Nicos grunted. Kat gave me an evil look. I thought of a

whole load of things I'd like to do for revenge, like ... shave Kat's precious eyebrows off when she was asleep and hide Nicos's phone in the freezer ... but I won't go into those now. I'd never do them anyway.

'Tut. Ignore them. You did the right thing, Lex.' Mum smiled and rubbed my knee. 'You shouldn't lie. You're a good girl.'

I liked it when she called me a good girl, but it didn't make me feel any better.

I *should* lie, I *shouldn't* lie – who am I meant to believe? It's so confusing. From the minute we're born, adults tell us we should never, ever lie. At disaster moments, they sit us down and say in a serious voice, 'I want you to tell me who cut half your sister's fringe off/trod chocolate cake into the carpet/threw the hamster in the paddling pool, and you won't get in trouble if you just tell the truth.'

But:

1) that's not true

2) parents lie all the time, and

3) my parents are worse than anyone I know.

I glared at the back of my parents' heads and all the

nonsense they told us came flooding back to me.

Most parents say that if you pull faces, the wind will change and you'll stay like that for ever. They say if you don't hurry up they'll leave without you, but they never do. On long car journeys, they promise you're almost there when you're still miles away, and they create this whole fantasy about tooth fairies collecting teeth from under your pillow.

But my parents? Well.

For a start, they told us robin redbreasts were Santa's mini-messengers and the one in the garden was watching our every move. If we whinged, broke our toys or didn't go to bed on time, the robin would flap to Lapland to tell Santa and we wouldn't get any presents. I didn't trust robins for years after that. To get me to eat calamari, Mum said it was fried rings of jellified marshmallow, when it's actually squid. She said if I didn't learn Greek, our ances-tors would haunt me, and that every time I got out of bed after lights out, a puppy died because of me.

As for my dad, he should win awards for the things he comes up with. He said you couldn't buy batteries for my flashing wailing toy car when it clearly had a battery

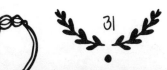

compartment, and that when the ice cream van starts playing music, it means it's only got salty ice cream left. He told us that if we said the word 'Dad' too many times at weekends, we'd disturb the peace and he'd get taken to prison, and worst of all, he said that our belly buttons were connected to our butts by a long hose in our gut, and if we untied our belly buttons, our butts would fall off.

See what I mean?

Even Yiayia, my grandma, who's very religious, says things that are suspicious. She points to her crucifixes and religious icons, which are all over her house, and tells us God is watching and if we're bad, he'll be angry and we'll go to hell. Now, I love Yiayia, but does God really care if I take the only whole ice lolly in the box and leave the broken ones for everyone else? And does hell even exist?

Whatever the answer is, lying is normal round here. Not that you can ever talk about it. You can't ask why *they're* allowed to lie and we're not. There are plenty of words for lies – I looked it up in the thesaurus once and wrote them down in my notebook. Some of them are funny, like:

32

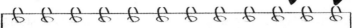

- bunkum
- baloney
- hooey
- eyewash
- hogwash
- flapdoodle
- piffle
- pish posh
- poppycock

and

- flim-flam

but 'lying' – well, that's a bad word. You get in trouble if you say someone's a liar, even if it's a kid, so you definitely don't want to say it about an adult. And there are all these layers and categories when it comes to lies. Fibbing is a nicer word, but means the same thing as lying, as far as I can tell. Then there are white lies and black lies, lies you *need* to tell so people don't get offended, and lies that stop people panicking. It's all so confusing.

Outside the car window, all kinds of people were crossing roads, walking down the high street, and waiting for buses. I gazed at them wondering, *When you get older, do you know the truth about lying or are you still just as clueless?*

I smacked my forehead on to the cold juddery glass and

closed my eyes. It was way too complicated to understand on one car journey. There were no rules around lying – not that I knew of, anyway. No two people gave you the same advice about whether you should lie or whether you shouldn't. And no heavenly voice in the sky thundered, 'Alexandra Efthimiou, for the biggest lie ever, you are now eternally DOOMED!'

Which is why, when it came to the moment I had to choose between telling the truth and telling the biggest lie I've ever told in my life – one that caused more trouble than I could have imagined and split my entire family apart – I had no idea what to do.

There should be some kind of handbook.

That's all I have to say.

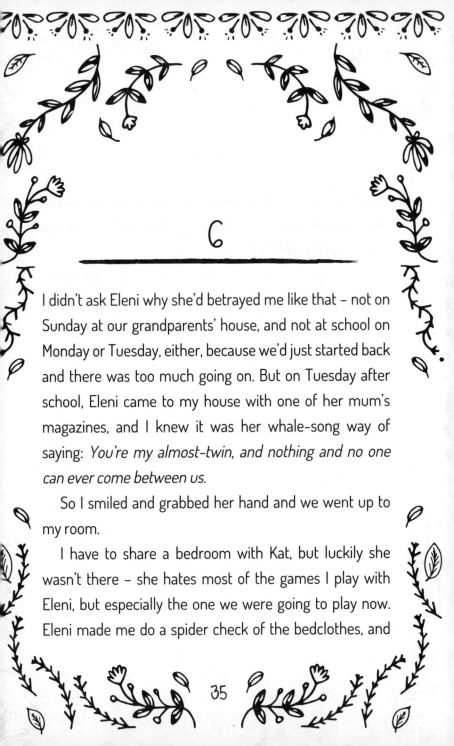

6

I didn't ask Eleni why she'd betrayed me like that – not on Sunday at our grandparents' house, and not at school on Monday or Tuesday, either, because we'd just started back and there was too much going on. But on Tuesday after school, Eleni came to my house with one of her mum's magazines, and I knew it was her whale-song way of saying: *You're my almost-twin, and nothing and no one can ever come between us.*

So I smiled and grabbed her hand and we went up to my room.

I have to share a bedroom with Kat, but luckily she wasn't there – she hates most of the games I play with Eleni, but especially the one we were going to play now. Eleni made me do a spider check of the bedclothes, and once I gave the all-clear, we lay on our stomachs and propped ourselves up with our elbows.

The magazine wasn't one of those cheap ones with slippery pages and photos of cheesy weddings. It was thick with heavy pages, full of adverts for designer clothes that only five people in the world can afford and no one wears in real life. Least no one *we've* ever seen. Just opening that magazine made us feel rich, stylish and fancy. We were *it*.

The models pouted a lot (which Eleni and I practised) and stood like bananas in petrol stations or the desert (which we also practised). Some of them were way too thin, though. Their bones stuck out, and that wasn't the shape we were going to be, judging by the women in our family. We were going to have boobs and bums and hips. And that was better because who wanted to starve and be a stick? Not anyone Greek, that's for sure.

We checked the prices and howled, '*Four thousand pounds*! For *shoes*! And look how UGLY they are! You could buy a mansion, a pool and a million jars of Nutella for that money!'

But the **real** reason we were looking at the magazines was to play our game. We'd been doing it for as long as we

could remember. It was called 'I'm her'. We played it all the time – not just when we read magazines. When we watched TV or saw someone wow and powerful and strong walking along the street, we'd whisper, 'I'm her,' to each other because those were the women we wanted to be.

Eleni squished closer to me, and put her feet between mine. Lying like that with our ankles entangled, sometimes I didn't know which feet belonged to me. Not that it mattered. She was me, and I was her, and the details didn't really bother us.

'Ready?' Eleni asked.

'Ready,' I replied.

She opened the front cover. The first photo was of a drop-dead gorgeous girl leading a drop-dead gorgeous life, trying to cross the road in New York in drop-dead gorgeous clothes.

'I'm her,' I said, quick as a whip.

'*I'm* her,' Eleni said a split-second after me.

'I said it first.'

Eleni squinted, pointed to the photo on the next page and said, 'So I'm *her*.'

37

'Fine. Be her. Why would I want to lie in a tree covered in leaves and massive jewellery?'

She frowned and said, 'Still her, though.'

We turned the page. The model in the next photo had long blonde hair, a bright silver jacket and five dogs on a leash.

'I'm her!' Eleni snapped. 'I said it first.'

'Fine.' I turned the page and slammed my finger down on the most stunning photo ever, making sure I got there before Eleni. 'I'M HER!'

Eleni said it too, but I was quicker. Anyway, I was so her. She was dark-haired and wow, wearing this red feathery ballgown with a train that swept behind her for about a mile.

'Jinx,' Eleni said. 'We're both her.'

'I said it first.'

She stuck her lips out and folded her arms. She wasn't taking that.

'I said it before you woke up this morning,' she said.

'I said it yesterday,' I replied.

'I said it last week.'

'I said it last year.'

'I said it when I was five.'

'I said it when I was one.'

'I said it before you were born.'

'You were born after me, Eleni!'

'So I said it before *I* was born.'

'You didn't have a mouth before you were born.'

'Yeah but I said it in my *head* when I was in my mum's belly.'

'I said it *before* I was in my mum's belly.'

'I said it in my last life.'

'I said it at the big bang.'

'I said it *before* the big bang.'

'MUM!' Kat yelled, walking into our bedroom. 'They're playing "I'm her" again!'

'Girls,' Mum said, coming in the bedroom holding plates of food. 'Stop that and eat something.'

Just before she left to go home, Eleni said, 'She's nice, Lexie.'

I knew who she was talking about but I pretended I didn't. I picked up our plates to take them downstairs, turned to face Eleni with the most innocent face I could

39

pull, and said, 'Who?'

'Anastasia. You'll like her. I invited her to my house so I can help her learn her story.'

I frowned. Every half term we had to learn a poem or story in Greek that we barely understood a word of. Then we had to recite it at Greek school to a whole audience of photo-taking, video-filming parents and grandparents who posted it on Facebook to humiliate us for all eternity.

'What? When's she coming?'

'After lunch on Sunday.'

I made a *sorry, what?* face. Sunday was our nail-polish-naming, food-sharing, notebook-writing, 'I'm her'-playing, TV-watching, homework-doing day.

'OK, but now you're lying, right?' I asked, feeling the need to check. 'Because . . . I honestly can't tell.'

Eleni laughed. 'Not lying. I don't lie ALL the time, you know. I'm only helping Stasi because she's bad at Greek.'

Stasi?

'It'll be fun. That's fine with you, isn't it?' Eleni asked.

All the things they'd told me were right and good since the day I was born, like God and the truth and heaven, flashed into my head, and I wanted to tell the truth. I really

did. Because it wasn't fine. Not even the tiniest bit fine. Not fine at all.

But I also remembered the keys in the sea and how everyone turned against me when I told the truth, and how it led to Eleni betraying me.

So instead of saying, 'No, actually. It's not OK with me,' I shrugged and said, 'Sure. Whatever.'

Because lying was totally normal. Everyone did it. Who even cared, right?

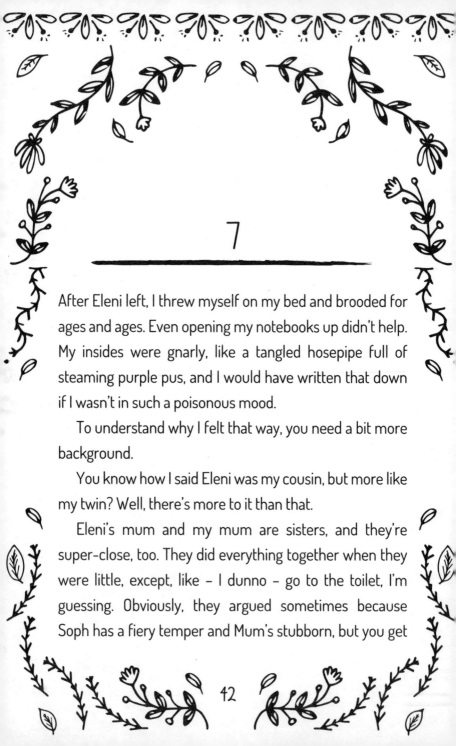

7

After Eleni left, I threw myself on my bed and brooded for ages and ages. Even opening my notebooks up didn't help. My insides were gnarly, like a tangled hosepipe full of steaming purple pus, and I would have written that down if I wasn't in such a poisonous mood.

To understand why I felt that way, you need a bit more background.

You know how I said Eleni was my cousin, but more like my twin? Well, there's more to it than that.

Eleni's mum and my mum are sisters, and they're super-close, too. They did everything together when they were little, except, like – I dunno – go to the toilet, I'm guessing. Obviously, they argued sometimes because Soph has a fiery temper and Mum's stubborn, but you get the idea. When they got married (eight months apart) they lived three roads away, which must have been creepy for Dad and Uncle Christos, but Dad said that was normal in Greek families and he liked to see sisters so close. And it helped that Dad and Uncle Christos got on so well. I wonder would have happened if they'd hated each other.

Anyhow, Mum had my sister, Katerina, six months before Aunt Sophia had Elias. Eighteen months later, Mum had Nicos, and three months after that, Auntie Soph had Kallie. But when it came to us, Mum and Aunt Sophia were pregnant at the same time and Eleni was born just five days after me. Which is one of the reasons we're almost twins.

'I was so exhausted when I visited Aunt Soph in hospital,' Mum's told me a thousand times. 'I put you in the transparent cot with Eleni – course, she didn't have a name yet – and climbed into Sophia's hospital bed with her. When the nurse came by, she couldn't understand why there were now two mothers asleep in the bed and two newborn babies asleep in the cot.'

Later that day, the doctors noticed Eleni had a prob-lem. A serious problem. She was going blue and wasn't breathing properly, so they ran some tests. They found she had something called hypoplastic left heart syndrome, which means the left side of her heart hadn't grown properly.

When she was one week old, Eleni had to have open-heart surgery.

Mum's told me that story a thousand times, too.

'After the surgery, on the seventh night of her life, we were all in the hospital, anxious and numb and waiting for news. The doctors came in looking serious and took Aunt Soph and Uncle C to one side. They said it wasn't looking good, and we should prepare for bad news. Eleni was so weak, they didn't think she'd make it to morning.'

Mum always pauses at that part. She takes a long breath and adds, 'That was the worst moment of our lives.' (I told you she was dramatic.) 'But later that night, a different doctor came in and said there was one more possibility. She'd read about it, and sometimes babies survived against the odds if another baby lay beside them. No one knew why. She said it was a gamble, but we were all so desperate to save Eleni by then that anything was worth a shot.

'So I lifted you out of your pram and handed you to the doctor. She carried you into the intensive care unit and laid you in the cot beside Eleni. She had a whole network of tubes all over her teeny body, and even though you were only twelve days old you were almost double her weight. The doctor laid you face to face, and we all watched from the window, holding hands.'

I know the rest of the story by heart.

After some time – maybe it was a few minutes, maybe more – I held my little hand out. I stretched my fingers towards Eleni's face and rested them on her cheek. I can't remember any of this, of course, but if I close my eyes and think about it, I can imagine it perfectly. All we hear is the other one breathing, and all we can feel is the warmth of the other one's skin. We have no idea that all around us machines are beeping, doctors are frowning, and parents are crying.

No one knows how, but Eleni made it through that night.

They took me out to feed and change me, but when they put me back, they placed us close together again.

Eleni made it through the next day, too.

45

And the next night.

And the day after that.

We've just taken it day by day ever since.

When she was strong enough to come out of hospital, they put us in the same pram. Aunt Soph thought it would be good for Eleni to have me close by – it would help her heal and feel safe. And it did. And she made me feel safe, too. I can't remember it, obviously, but I know it's true because she still does.

We did everything together after that. We have hundreds of photos of us in the same pram – my scribble of curly hair on one side and her fair silky head on the other. And chewing on each other's hands, asleep with our heads touching, screaming in paddling pools, making sandcastles, taking our first steps and having birthday parties together.

Our families would go into each other's houses all the time with pots of food, and every year we'd all go to my grandparents' house with fifty other members of my big loud mad family for Christmas and Easter (and Easter is big for Greeks). Eleni and I were always together. Always.

Eleni had to have two more operations, one when she was five months and one when she was two. Only six in ten babies survive all three of those operations, so now everyone calls her the Miracle Baby and treats her as if she's made of glass. She gets away with being naughty and cheeky, and they all love her. Not just in our family but in the whole community. Like she's a celebrity.

Her condition means she still has to be careful because her heart isn't as strong as other people's. She goes to the cardiologist all the time for check-ups and she can't do the stuff kids usually do. So we do other things, like make up games and make each other laugh. Since we were babies, there hasn't been anything Eleni and I have had to do on our own. We're like one plant with two flowers, or a two-headed cat (or something).

So saying she's my cousin doesn't really sound right.

I just use the word 'cousin' because there isn't a better one yet.

47

8

That's why Eleni being friends with Anastasia was bothering me so much. They made each other laugh and I started to wonder whether I was funny enough. I didn't make Eleni laugh like that. But it was also the first time Eleni had ever taken someone else's side and not mine, and now that I'd lied to my almost-twin, who I loved more than anyone, the world had changed. Just a little bit. But all the same, now it felt completely different.

So different, in fact, that on Sunday at church (we have to go every week or the world will melt or something), I gazed at the high ceilings, the stained glass, the icons and the altar, and felt further away from good and holy than I'd ever felt before. I saw Anastasia near the back with her parents, and my stomach became a gnarly hosepipe of poisonous pus again. The priest waved around this incense holder with jingly bells and talked really fast in an ancient Greek language no one understands, not even my parents, and when the service was over, we went up the grey carpeted stairs to Greek school.

I was feeling pretty bad already, but then, as I stood in the corridor, waiting for Eleni to come out of the toilet, Anastasia, wearing a peach top and orange shorts, walked past me like I was a wall. Like I wasn't standing right there. Like this wasn't MY home and MY neighbourhood she'd just turned up in. I'd been going to that church all my life! I started Greek school when I was four and I was nearly eleven now! I knew everybody, and everybody knew me. Our parents were all friends and our grandparents grew up in the same town/village/house/room back in Cyprus. Even our Greek teacher, Kyria Maria, was Mum's cousin's husband's sister.

It wasn't the same safe world that I knew any more. People like Anastasia could turn up and change everything.

I ground my teeth. *Fine*, I thought. *You want to be like that? I might have **told** on you, but it wasn't **me** who threw car keys in the sea.*

49

Just then, Eleni came out of the toilet. I was about to tell her what had happened when Anastasia came over to us. In two seconds flat, they were laughing about the story Anastasia had to learn at Eleni's house, and ignoring me like I wasn't standing right there beside them.

'My Greek's so bad!' Anastasia screeched.

'You need this for luck,' Eleni said, and slipped a friendship bracelet off her wrist.

I scowled as Anastasia put it on. She glanced at me, and then beamed at Eleni, which really annoyed me. With heat rising like flames licking my face, I went into the classroom and sat where Eleni and I always sat – at the front on the right. While I waited for Eleni to come in, I tried to stop evil thoughts brewing, seeing as I was still in church and everything.

When our teacher, Kyria Maria, walked into the room, Eleni came and sat beside me, which made me feel victorious. But then Eleni beckoned to Anastasia. 'Come and sit here,' she said, shifting her chair over and squashing me. I glared at the table and ground my teeth. On the piece of paper Kyria Maria always had ready on the table, I wrote:

50

> Noooooooooo!!!!!!!!!

Eleni looked at me and frowned. Then she wrote:

> What? Don't be like that. She's nice.

I wanted to write:
She's **not nice**.
She threw our keys in the sea.
She's *ignoring* me.
She wants to get in the middle of us.
I DON'T LIKE HER!

But I didn't. Eleni was my twin. She'd get it, surely. And if not, we always had whale song.

'It's OK, I'll sit here,' Anastasia said, pulling out a chair beside Demi Kolitsas. 'Maybe next week,' she added with a smile. And then class started.

9

At break, Eleni skipped over to the window where Anastasia was tying her hair back and said excitedly, 'Yay! You're coming today!' Then she turned to me, beckoned with her hand and said, 'Lexie, come.'

I hauled myself up from the chair, slouched over and stood beside them but kept my eyes looking out of the window. It was a dull, fuzzy day and the sky looked like the inside of a vacuum cleaner bag. By the side of the road, a cross-looking lady in a red coat was waiting with a plastic bag over her hand next to a small, hairy dog that was doing number twos. It wasn't the best view in the world, I was thinking, when Eleni poked me and said, 'You're coming to my house as well this afternoon. After we've finished doing the story. OK? We're all going to be friends.'

Anastasia's mouth twisted into something that was supposed to be a smile but I knew it wasn't. Or maybe it was. Maybe she *was* actually really nice and I had it all wrong. But then she blinked slow and hard as if her eyes hurt to look at me and turned her shoulder so she was half-facing the other way. 'Yeah, come, but we might finish late,' she said. 'We'll be having so much fun we won't be able to concentrate on the story.'

Eleni laughed and said, 'Lexie can join in. And then we'll watch TV and eat popcorn.'

Anastasia flashed a toothy smile, and twisted Eleni's friendship bracelet around on her wrist.

I tried to smile back but my mouth wasn't happy about it and it made a yank like I had toothache. Not that either of them noticed. I turned back to the window and carried on looking at the woman scooping up the dog poop. Because even though it wasn't a very nice sight, it was still better than looking at Anastasia.

On Sundays after Greek school, we eat lunch at Yiayia and Pappou's house. Every Sunday. Without fail. Other kids I know go to birthday parties, do sports or go shopping on

Sundays. For us, that's not an option. We go to my grand-parents' house to eat. All of us. Every week. If someone didn't come, they'd get massively offended and it would be the biggest deal ever. You just didn't miss it and that was that.

Yiayia and Pappou's house looked like the inside of a church, with crucifixes on the walls and icons of Jesus and the Virgin Maria everywhere. There was a special room for entertaining called a *saloni*, with quilts over the furniture to keep it clean and hundreds of framed photos of Yiayia and Pappou's children graduating and getting married and of their grandchildren smiling with no teeth. We weren't allowed to sit there, and we were only allowed to eat at the kitchen table, which had a lace cloth on it like a big doily and a bowl of fruit in the middle that got taken off when we sat down to eat. Which was every time we walked in the door.

Sunday lunch was something special, though. They used their best china and glasses, and the house smelt amazing, even from outside the door. We always started with *avgolemono* (egg-and-lemon-flavoured chicken soup), then chips and crumbed chicken, *fasolia*

(beans and potatoes in tomato sauce), lamb (in different ways every week), and sometimes fish and *dolmades* (stuffed vine leaves), too. Afterwards, we had fruit, Yiayia's amazing cinnamon cake and *koulourakia* (plaited shortbreads). If you visited Yiayia and didn't eat, she'd go on and on about it for ever. The food was delicious, anyway – why would you not eat? You'd just better be hungry when you turned up, because there was lots of it.

Sunday lunch is one of three billion Greek traditions you inherit when you're born and have to continue in your own house for all eternity or your life is just not worth living. Mum was getting more into traditions by then, too, for some reason. Maybe because she was getting old. Don't tell her I said that or she'll kill me, because she keeps saying forty-four isn't old. But it kind of is if you start putting lacy tablecloths under plastic wipeable covers.

'Why have you started putting one of these on our table at home?' I asked her when I saw the one at Yiayia's house. We'd just finished eating and I was writing out some words for 'cousin' in my notebook.

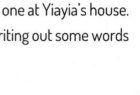

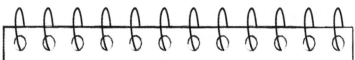

Kallie-gator: a cousin who pinches you hard at Greek school to get her revenge.

Traitorella: a cousin who spends too much time with another girl who isn't her twin.

Things like that.

'It's traditional,' Mum said. 'Traditions are important.'

Dad looked at the tablecloth and then at me. 'What, like putting a giant doily on the table? And cutting a piece of a baby's hair off to protect it from evil?' he straddled a chair and put his coffee on the giant doily.

Mum crossed her arms. 'What's wrong with that?'

Dad burst out laughing. I could have told him that was a bad move. 'How can cutting a bit of hair off protect you from—'

'Not everything is logical,' Mum snapped, and she took Dad's coffee away and washed the cup, even though he hadn't finished drinking it.

56

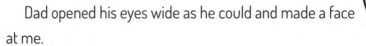

Dad opened his eyes wide as he could and made a face at me.

I grinned, but Mum was right. Plenty of things weren't logical. Like how Yiayia has blue glass eyeballs hanging around her house and garden, and cactuses at the front door to ward off the evil eye. She does a little 'tut tut' like she's spitting if someone pays her a compliment, and if she sees shoes upside down with the soles showing, she says '*skorda*' ('garlic') under her breath. Then she spits a couple of times and turns them the right way up. And that's not even all of it.

According to Yiayia, if it's traditional, you do it. Even if it makes no sense.

Six decades from now, when I'm a world-famous dictionary writer, I'll make up a hundred words for 'tradition', including 'stupid ones that no one gets'.

But then again, maybe I'll just leave out the word 'tradition' completely.

Especially after what happened next.

10

After lunch, we went home and, to pass the time, I wrote a bit more in my notebook until I could go to Eleni's. My brain felt like a giant chainsaw buzzing in my skull, so I wrote that down. On her bed, my sister's huge padded bra looked like a mutant crustacean ready to pounce, so I wrote that down. And my brother was playing music that sounded like a dizzy horse had fallen into a row of metal dustbins, so I wrote that down, too.

Then I told Mum I'd finished my homework, which was almost true, and Dad dropped me at Eleni's house.

Eleni and Anastasia had finished the story for Greek school and were watching the first *Harry Potter* on TV, which Eleni and I knew pretty much by heart. Eleni kept saying the lines and looking at Anastasia, but Anastasia

didn't seem to know them. I was mouthing them silently, because how can you not when you know something that well? Not that Eleni noticed. Anastasia was sitting super-close to Eleni on the sofa, which made me want to growl like a gnashy dog but I controlled myself. I sat on the other end of the sofa with Eleni in the middle and Anastasia at the end.

Then Anastasia, not watching TV at all, tucked her feet under Eleni and said, 'Let's have a sleepover at my house next weekend. We can make cookies and do makeovers on each other.'

She didn't invite me. I acted as if it didn't bother me, because that's how you're supposed to behave. Which means the way you act can be a lie as well.

'OK. Can you come, Lexie?' Eleni asked, holding her hand out to me. I took it, but I was wincing. Did I want to go? Did I want to be left out? Which was worse?

I was still wondering about that when there was a close-up of Harry Potter's scar, which made Anastasia ask Eleni about hers.

Now, Eleni's scar is like a sacred, frozen river running across her chest. No one gets to see except family. It's

proof of how hard she had to fight just to stay here. With me. With all of us. But mainly with me. Mum says it's the line left behind when the string trying to pull her up to heaven broke, but to me, it's where I was cut away, making us into two people when we were really one.

'I want to see it!' Anastasia said, clapping excitedly like it was a new gadget or something. I was about to snap, 'Well, you can't!' when Eleni gently raised her yellow long-sleeved T-shirt with 'Talk to the Hand' written on the front.

Eleni wasn't blue any more but she was still pale and skinny. Under her shirt, she had a white crop top on, and the scar ran from above it, near her neck, to underneath it, by her belly button. Anastasia gasped and whispered, 'Wowwww.' She ran her finger along the trail of rippled shiny skin and added, 'That is so cool!'

I sucked air into my lungs. One thing that scar was not was cool. Eleni nearly died. She still could. And the thought of that made my insides clamp together.

'Yeah,' Eleni said, looking a little unsure because she knew as well as I did that 'cool' wasn't even close to what that scar stood for. 'I guess it is.'

'Oh. My. God,' Anastasia said. 'I just had an idea! We

could pretend we're, like, twins or something and that's where we were cut apart!'

That did it.

With my eyes scorching, I leapt out of the chair and bolted from the room. Struggling to breathe, I grabbed my coat from the hook and flung open the front door. Then I sprinted down the road like I was being chased by a lion, my legs slamming on the paving stones, pushing, pushing, pushing me away from there. Tears streamed down my face and I breathed loudly and quickly so I wouldn't scream. I bolted all the way home, which isn't far but I was absolutely no way allowed to walk it on my own.

When I got to our front door I slammed against it, gasping for air and trying not to cry. I hammered on it and eventually, Kat opened it, staring at her phone. She turned her back on me and walked down the hall, saying, 'OK. Keep your hair on.'

'Why're you back?' Mum barked from the sitting room. 'Didn't come on your own, did you?'

I ran up the stairs, panting, 'Elias . . . walked me . . . to the end of the road. And I . . . I ran the rest!' Which was a lie I told to my own mother.

'He's supposed to walk you to the door!' Mum came out and stood at the foot of the bannisters. I raced upstairs so she wouldn't see my face.

'You crying?' she hollered in her usual caring, gentle, sensitive way.

I bit my lip.

'Lex! Why're you crying?'

'I – er – I forgot,' I said, thinking quickly but still not looking at her. 'I've got more homework. Don't shout at me! I'll do it now!'

'Oh my God!' she yelled with a laugh. 'Calm down, will you? Me? Shout? As if.'

Then she cracked up because she knows she's the world's biggest shouter. She shouts even when she's saying hello to the sweet old lady two doors away. 'Just don't lie about it next time,' she added.

And I thought, *Hah*.

I wouldn't count on it.

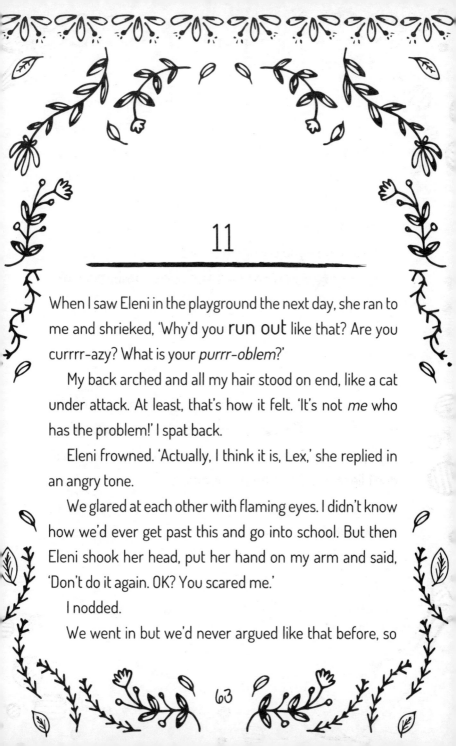

11

When I saw Eleni in the playground the next day, she ran to me and shrieked, 'Why'd you **run out** like that? Are you currrr-azy? What is your *purrr-oblem*?'

My back arched and all my hair stood on end, like a cat under attack. At least, that's how it felt. 'It's not *me* who has the problem!' I spat back.

Eleni frowned. 'Actually, I think it is, Lex,' she replied in an angry tone.

We glared at each other with flaming eyes. I didn't know how we'd ever get past this and go into school. But then Eleni shook her head, put her hand on my arm and said, 'Don't do it again. OK? You scared me.'

I nodded.

We went in but we'd never argued like that before, so

we were both in shock for the rest of the day.

Anastasia went to a different school to us so I didn't see her that week, but I know Eleni did because she told me. Anastasia went to Eleni's house again after school on Wednesday, and Aunt Soph and Anastasia's mother had made plans to go to Hampton Court at the weekend. I'd never been to Hampton Court. I wanted to go, but not with Anastasia. At least they weren't having the sleepover, though. Anastasia's uncle was coming to visit so they'd changed it to another weekend.

Still.

Every night that week, before I went to sleep, I lay staring at the ceiling with my guts in a knot. And because it was night and I was home in my own bed, Eleni wasn't there to remind me that barbequed marshmallows are squishy in the middle and crispy on the outside, or that cosy cocoons contain snoozing caterpillars that are in for a big shock when they break out.

After an hour of not sleeping, I turned on my torch and opened my notebook. A couple of weeks before we'd jotted down a new list of things that make us happy.

<u>Good things. Sunday 30 August.</u>
- Birthday parties (especially going-home bags)
- Messages written in secret code
- Popping bubble wrap
- Going to the circus
- Walking in puddles with wellies on
- Glow-in-the-dark stars on the ceiling
- Ice lollies on very hot days (not broken ones from Pappou's freezer)
- Turtles
- Buried treasure and pirate maps
- Cute dogs
- Aquariums - especially with clown fish

But even reading that didn't make me feel any better. It just made me miss Eleni more.

A couple of weeks later, after Eleni went to Hampton Court with Anastasia (and had a totally amazing time – I know because Eleni told me all about it), Uncle Dimitri got

65

us all together in Pappou's house on Saturday afternoon, and announced that he was getting engaged to Christina, his girlfriend.

We were so excited, we screamed, and we weren't the only ones. Yiayia had wanted Dimitri to get married since he was like eighteen or something and now he was thirty-four, which is *really* old. Yiayia didn't stop going about it, and she was so happy, she threw an engagement party that very night to celebrate. Not a big one – more like a family gathering in Yiayia and Pappou's house. But we all love parties so we didn't care.

And, even better, we had a wedding to look forward to! Eleni and I would be bridesmaids! We'd spend all our evenings and weekends together planning for it and making notes in our notebooks and playing 'I'm her' and Anastasia wouldn't be part of any of it.

Everything would be fine from now to eternity, and that was the best feeling ever.

12

Mum and Soph spent the rest of the afternoon getting ready in my mum and dad's bedroom. Mum's dressing table was covered in jars of brushes, boxes of nail varnish, palettes and palettes of eyeshadows, circles of bronzers and highlighters, and who knows what else. The hairdryer and tongs were plugged in and ready to roll (haha) and sparkly dresses were hanging on the wardrobe doors. Ten pairs of heels were sprawled across the floor, and they were all tried on, not only by my mum and Sophia to see which ones matched their dresses best, but also by Eleni and me, just for the fun of it.

Mum and Soph always got dressed up like this. They could go to the Oscars and look like they were supposed to be there. They even got dressed up for funerals, which

I know about now, because I've seen them at one. Unfortunately. But we'll get to the funeral later. Right then, we were getting ready for a party.

Eleni and I sat propped up on pillows on the bed, watching. Mum was wearing a white satin dressing gown with Japanese writing on it and she smelt of lychee or mango or something fruity, thanks to her luxury after-spa body cream. Her long dark hair was wound in red hair rollers and she had an arch of gold glitter just above the thick black flick of her eyeliner. Eleni thought she looked glamorous. I thought she looked like an alien.

Long strips of toilet paper were laced between Mum's toes to separate them because she'd just painted her toenails Baby Poo Cappuccino (or at least, that was what Eleni and I called it). Aunt Soph sat on a stool, hunched over, stroking stripes of shiny red varnish on to my mum's fingers. Mum can't paint her right hand: Aunt Soph always does it for her. Meanwhile, Eleni and I were naming the new nail polish.

'Looks like a thick lick of blood,' I whispered to Eleni, and then I paused. 'Blood Lick?'

Eleni squinted. 'Blood-Stained Vampire Lick.'

My eyes widened. It was good. But not quite right. 'Neck Blood Vamp Lick.'

'*Fresh* Blood Vamp Lick.'

I raised my hand, we high-fived and I wrote it in the notebook before we forgot. 'Fresh Blood Vamp Lick' it was. Nice.

'This is **mine**,' Mum said, picking up a dark brown nail varnish. She looked at Aunt Soph. 'Why's it in *your* nail varnish box?'

'Borrowed it,' Aunt Soph said, 'for that work do.'

'Tut. Why d'you always nick my stuff? My furry jacket, my sofa blanket and now this. I looked everywhere for that sofa blanket.'

Aunt Soph laughed. 'We left late! Eleni was cold. I wrapped her in it.'

'So bring it back! Your house is full of my stuff!'

'Eleni was cold!' Aunt Soph yelled, but she was grinning. 'I'll bring it back tomorrow.'

Mum took the nail varnish out of Aunt Soph's box and put it on her dressing table, saying, 'And I'll have that back, thank you. What are you like?'

Eleni and I wanted to get our nails painted too, but we

had to wait. Aunt Soph had put curlers in our hair and while she painted Mum's nails, Eleni and I were choosing the best colours in an eye shadow palette. Not to wear. Just for fun.

'Midnight Blue,' I said. 'And Midas Gold.'

'Heavy Metal,' Eleni said. 'And Unicorn Poo.'

'That's not what it's called. It's called Pretty in Pink.'

'Looks like unicorn poo. I've renamed it.'

I grinned. Eleni and I loved times like these. We were going to wear dresses that looked like cloud puffs, eat *kataifi* until we felt sick and stay up late. And because it was a family do, Anastasia wasn't going to be there.

The world was a happy place again.

On top of that, Uncle Dimitri was getting married! MARRIED! Even though he was old! My parents got married when they were twenty-two. Uncle Dimitri had grey hairs and Christina still wanted to marry him!

Weird.

Dad was watching the Crystal Palace game on TV with Uncle Christos, but he knew better than to come upstairs at times like these. He'd end up with his eyebrows plucked and his hair blow-dried, so he stayed downstairs, making

jokes no one except Uncle C laughed at, while Uncle C did a commentary the whole way through that drove everyone crazy, including Dad.

When we'd finished choosing the best eye shadows, we opened a magazine and started playing 'I'm her' until Mum said, 'Girls, cut it out will you? What colour nail polish d'you want?'

'Dead Princess Milkshake!' we yelled at the same time, and pointed towards the pink.

13

We all drove back to Pappou and Yiayia's house. Dad drove in his car but Eleni and I sat together in Uncle C's big jeep. We squealed excitedly all the way (driving Kallie mad) and when we arrived, Eleni and I scrambled out in our favourite clothes.

It was a warm evening, even though it was the end of September. It wasn't exactly Cyprus in August or anything, but the double doors to the garden were wide open, and there were adults already standing between the toilets, chatting and laughing.

Yes, I did say toilets.

See, Pappou and Yiayia have a beautiful garden because Pappou spends all his time out there planting flowers and vegetables, but it has this really embarrassing

feature. Pappou worked in the building trade before he retired, and don't ask me why, but he kept the toilets people threw out when they did renovations. He's lined about twenty of them along both sides of the path in his garden and he uses them as flowerpots. His garden looks like a toilet graveyard. And family and friends were standing around them in fancy dresses and clean shirts, holding wine glasses. It was so freaky.

Christina came out in a shimmery blue dress and stood between Uncle Dimitri and a toilet. Except for the toilet, she looked like a movie star. Her long dark hair hung in loose curls, her big blue eyes shone and her huge smile showed perfect teeth.

'I'm her!' Eleni and I said at the same time.

She wasn't like the girls in the magazines: she was real and she was Greek and she wasn't standing like a banana with her bones sticking out. On top of that, she was a daring doctor who took action in warzones to save lives (OK, she was a GP in Norwood, but still). We'd never wanted to be anyone as much as we wanted to be her.

'We're *both* her,' I said, and Eleni nodded.

Mum walked past saying, 'Girls, stop that and eat

something,' and handed us a plate of food a starving grizzly bear wouldn't have finished on its own.

Eleni took a mini *spanakopita* (spinach and feta pie), bit a small piece off, then handed it to me and I took a bite.

I handed it back and she took a bite.

She passed it to me and I took a bite.

She took a bite.

I took a bite.

She took a bite.

We passed it wordlessly between us as the pie got smaller and smaller and flakes of pastry fell on the rug. Our bites turned into nibbles, and then tiny weeny pecks. By then it was so incy we could hardly pass or bite it, but we kept trying until it was too small to bite any more and the microscopic speck that was left dissolved into nothing on my lips.

Whoever ate the last part was the greedy one. It was usually Eleni because I was so good at it, but not this time. So Eleni got to say it: 'Greedy.'

Mum yelled, 'What are you doing? Do you think there isn't enough or something? Have one each! Have two each! Why are you *sharing*?'

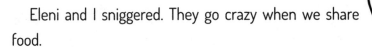

Eleni and I sniggered. They go crazy when we share food.

All evening, Yiayia couldn't stop hugging Dimitri and Christina. 'You make me **happiest** mother in all the whole world,' she kept saying. 'I pray **every day** – I pray for my boy he get marry to **good Greek girl**. And God he listen to my prayers and he give **you**. **Best** girl ever. I . . . **so happy** . . . you . . . will be my . . . **daughter**.'

And then she cried for the rest of the evening like she was going away for ever and she'd never see him again.

Which, looking back, was kind of strange.

I wonder if she knew.

14

When it got late and the adults didn't look like they were ending the party any time soon, Yiayia took Eleni and me to bed. Yiayia and Pappou only lived ten minutes away from us but we liked staying there. Yiayia made it fun. She let us ask her a million questions about when she was young and met Pappou and how handsome he was, and we sat in her bed with her and watched black-and-white movies and she kept bringing us snacks like we were queens.

We scaled the stairs drowsily, holding little bags of *koufeta*, which are sugar-coated almonds. Apparently, if you put them under your pillow, you dream of your prince. Eleni and I wanted to see if it worked, and if we had princes, what they looked like. We figured if we didn't like

the princes we dreamt of, we'd go down and get other bags of *koufeta* and try to dream of different princes, but we weren't sure if that was allowed.

Yiayia was tired, too. We climbed on to her bed, sleepy and full of food, and watched her pull her dress over her blow-dried hair, which was beige, tough and thick like wire. She had dark red fingernails at the end of her hands, which were so veiny, they looked like alien hands. Everything about her was interesting. Eleni and I could have investigated her body and her belongings for hours. We were fascinated by her saggy skin and amazed that ours would do the same when we were old. We liked Yiayia's elbows best. She didn't mind when we pulled the skin out to do the stretch test, even though our mums told us to stop doing it ages ago. The skin on her elbows was thick and rubbery – it didn't spring back like ours did. It stayed sticking out like unelasticated dough or a strange blobby skin creature.

We didn't tell Yiayia that.

She put on her long pink nightdress, opened her wardrobe and lifted her jewellery box off the shelf. It was rectangular and wooden, with shiny pearly swirliness

77

covering the inside, and had three tiers of rings and gems and trinkets.

'Ooh. Mini treasure chest. Can we see it?' Eleni asked.

'Is now the bedtime,' Yiayia said, taking off her earrings and dropping them in.

'*Parakalo*?' (That means 'please' in Greek.) 'Just for one minute and five seconds.'

Yiayia looked at Eleni and her eyes creased in a web of smiley wrinkles. 'One minute and five seconds? *Entaksi*.' (That means 'OK'.) 'But no more.'

Eleni nodded eagerly. 'Not a minute-second longer.'

'It's a *milli*second,' I told her, but Eleni ignored me. She was right, though: 'minute-second' sounded miles better.

Yiayia carefully handed us the box and we gazed at it, picking up in turn the brooches (ugly), the gold bracelets (heavy), the old-fashioned rings with stones set in them like flower petals (too big for every one of our fingers) and the crucifix necklaces (holy). Yiayia had a story for every one of them, but she was tired now and our minute-and-five-seconds was running out fast, so we didn't ask her to tell them.

'Yiayia? Where's the wedding necklace?' I asked.

'Ah,' she said, winking. 'I not keep it here now.'

'How come?' Eleni asked.

'I keep it in other place. Secret place.'

'Can we see it?' I asked.

'You say me one minute and five seconds.'

'Yeah, but that was for the jewellery box,' I said. 'This is different. Please? Only for . . . thirty-seven seconds.'

'Thirty-seven seconds?' Yiayia laughed loudly. 'You girls. So funny. You want see it?'

'YES!' we both yelled.

'But thirty-seven second only—' she said, holding up her finger.

'OK,' I said, although Eleni was looking at me as if that wasn't long enough.

'—and then bed.'

'OK, Yiayia,' Eleni said. 'It's a deal.'

'Yes,' Yiayia said, edging off the side of bed where she'd been sitting, 'Yes. You right. Is veerrrrry important. The people who not knowing where is it they are come from, is like tree what not have the root.'

Eleni and I looked at each other excitedly because in our family, we had this very special family heirloom necklace. It had been worn by the women at their weddings for generations. My great-great-grandmother's father had bought it for her wedding day from a Middle Eastern trader, and she'd passed it down, so my great-grandma and all her sisters wore it at their weddings, and then Yiayia and her sisters. My mother and Aunt Sophia wore it at theirs, and Christina would wear it when she married Uncle Dimitri.

The tradition was that although everyone got to wear it, it was passed down to the oldest daughter in the family, so Yiayia got it after her mother died, and after Yiayia died, it'd be passed to my mum, and then she'd pass it to my sister Katerina and she'd give it to *her* oldest daughter. We knew it wasn't ever going to belong to Eleni or me, but we'd get to wear it at our weddings, like all the other women in our family. And we knew how special it was to all of us.

Yiayia put her jewellery box away, closing the treasures inside the shiny lid.

'I show you wedding necklace,' she said, 'but close the eyes. And not pooping.'

We giggled. 'She means peeping,' Eleni said, but I knew that already.

We clapped our fingers over our eyes but we both pooped through the gaps. I know this because I looked at Eleni and she looked at me and we giggled again silently but just using our shoulders this time. *This is fun!* we both said in whale song.

Yiayia shuffled in her slippers to the chest of drawers and said, 'No look!'

'We're no looking!' we said, even though we totally were. Before, I would have closed my eyes for sure, but now I kept them open. Lying is easy when you get used to it.

She opened the third drawer from the bottom, rummaged around at the back, then took out a dark cloth cover from underneath some clothes. Then she closed the drawer, came back to the bed and said, '*Entaksi.* Open eyes now.'

She laid it next to us, opened the gold clasp and unfolded the cloth.

15

Eleni and I gasped. We'd seen the necklace before but we'd forgotten how gorgeous it was. It was an orangey-gold Greek cross about three centimetres high, engraved with small swirly lines, and it had a dark, pinkish ruby in the middle. Each of the four ends of the cross looked like the tops of love hearts, curvy and divided into two parts – which made sense, seeing as it was a wedding necklace.

'Twenty-four carats this gold,' Yiayia said, but we didn't understand why gold would be made of carrots.

'Soooo beautiful,' Eleni cooed, opening her nostrils wide so you could see the white bony outline of her nose.

'So beautiful and so *old*,' I said. Just looking at it was like opening a door to a distant world.

'Like a thousand hundred years or something,' Eleni

said, getting the numbers the wrong way around as usual. Which was weird considering she liked counting so much.

Yiayia put her lined face close to ours so we could see how her red lipstick had leaked into the earthquake cracks at the edges of her lips. Her breath smelt a bit like clothes in a charity shop, and it mingled with the perfume she always wore, which I think was roses.

'This necklace she survive war with Turkey and the Germans and in hard, hard time when they,' (she meant the people in the past) 'not have food and they need money so bad, my Pappou he say he want sell it. But my Yiayia clever. She hide it. She keep necklace safe so she can give it to my mother. And my mother she hide it, too. They take care of it for give they daughters so they can wear it on the day of the wedding day.' Eleni and I grinned at each other because Yiayia's English was funny. 'Because of this special womens,' Yiayia went on, 'this necklace still here with us now. This is big big miracle. Very special these womens. They are know what is it important in the  life. And this – this in you blood.'

'Imagine,' I said to Eleni, 'what our blood must look like under a microscope.'

83

She chuckled. 'And imagine. All those women wore it at their weddings, and one day, we're going to wear it, too. And they're all dead now,' her voice went quiet and low, 'and the necklace is still alive.'

I grinned. Typical Eleni. It wasn't creepy to us, though: it made it kind of magical.

'I happy you like,' Yiayia said. 'Very special, this necklace. Now even more than before.'

'What do you mean?' I asked, shifting my eyes from the necklace to Yiayia.

She looked at both of us cautiously, then said, 'I tell you big big secret. OK?'

We nodded quickly. We liked secrets.

'This necklace, my leeettle Eleni, I keep it for you.'

I stared at Yiayia and then at Eleni. That wasn't the tradition. That necklace was supposed to be given to my mum, and then she'd pass it on to Katerina – unless Kat died in a terrible, tragic accident, in which case it would come to me. Which I wasn't hoping for, obviously, but if it happened I wouldn't say no. Don't tell Katerina that.

'But Yiayia—' Eleni began, frowning.

'Oh, yessss, yessss, I knooow. I must to give to oldest

daughter. Is tradition. And tradition is verrry important. If we no have tradition, then who are we?' She paused. 'But this time, no. This necklace survive war and very hard time, and you, Eleni-*mou*, you do, too.'

I wrinkled my nose in confusion. Eleni hadn't been in a war. What was Yiayia talking about?

'When you come in this world,' Yiayia went on, looking at Eleni, 'you so smaaaall, so sweeeeet, but you heart it's no good. I say Pappou, iss no possible make so big operation on so small baby. But they open you up like chicken on butcher table. And I pray – I pray every night and every day for ask God have mercy on you. I look through the window at you in small box in the special care and I beg you, "Little Eleni, stay here with us. You have beautiful life ahead of you." And all I hear is beep beep of machine. The doctors they whisper and the nurses, they look too much serious and I know the true. Probably you will die. And I cry because this smaaaall baby, she my granddaughter, and my heart full of love. So I say you, "Little Eleni-*mou*, I make deal with you, OK? You stay here with us, I give *you* the necklace. I keep it for you for when you big and strong, and you meet a nice Greek boy and you marry with him.

But you must to stay with us. Please. Stay with us, little Eleni.'"

She paused. Both of us were staring at her with our mouths open.

'And you live.'

Yiayia had tears in her eyes by this point, but so did we. It was like a story from a book, only better because it was true and about us.

Then Yiayia smiled at Eleni. 'I think you live only for this,' she said, holding up the necklace with a wink. 'You want the wedding necklace. And I understand you. It is verrrry beautiful.'

Eleni and I laughed.

'A promise,' Yiayia said with her finger pointing up, 'is a promise. So I change the tradition. I'm allowed. Don't worry. I speak with God and He tell me it's OK. He talk with me all the time – no, really. Why you laugh? It's true. Christina will wear it when she marry my Dimitri, and Katerina and Kallie when they get married, and both of you,' she said, looking from me to Eleni, 'but the necklace it is for Eleni, for being a good baby and staying alive.'

Eleni and I looked at each other with wide open eyes. I

86

felt a little left out, of course, because Eleni always got extra love and attention because of her heart. But I was also worried.

Yiayia wrapped the necklace back up, told us to close our eyes, and put it in her drawer. 'This our secret, OK?' she whispered, turning to us.

We nodded and said, 'OK,' even though suddenly it didn't feel very OK. All my skin was prickling and my mouth went dry, like I'd just had a glass of tumble-dried sand mixed with cranberry juice.

What would my mum think about this?

16

Yiayia shuffled towards us in her pink fluffy slippers, sat on the end of the bed and said, 'Girls. My heart is happy, you know why? Because my boy, my only son, he get marry. And his wife is beautiful girl – not only outside, she beautiful inside. And she is doctor. Like you will be, too. My grandchildren they will not make clothes in a Greek factory like I do when I come to England.'

'Actually, I'm going to write dictionaries,' I said. I'm not sure why, but no one in my family is that keen about me being a dictionary writer.

'You are going … to be … doctor.'

'Who writes dictionaries.'

'In your spare time. If you have. First you learn to cook Greek food and you have babies.'

Eleni and I looked at each other and made OMG faces.

'My son love her and she love him, and for this I say thank you to God with all of my heart. Girls, soon we have wedding.' She jiggled her shoulders like a five-year-old. Uncle Dimitri's wedding was next summer – a whole year away! – which didn't feel like soon to us. It felt like forever. We wanted it to be next week! Than Yiayia added, 'I wait for this day long time. But now I tired and you tired, too. So-u. Bed.'

Eleni and I groaned, crept off her bed and shuffled into the spare room. We put our pyjamas on, brushed our teeth in Yiayia's yellow bathroom and curled up together in one single bed (even though the spare room had two), placing the *koufeta* under our pillow so we'd dream about our princes. Then we lay like spoons, with my stomach resting against her back. Downstairs, we could hear voices and laughter through the open doors, and someone singing along to a famous Greek song.

'Imagine getting married!' Eleni whispered in the dark. 'Do you think we even will?'

'Sure,' I said. 'We'll get married at the same time, maybe

even have a double wedding – probably to another pair of cousins—'

'Or brothers.'

'—or brothers. You can wear the necklace for the first half of the wedding and I'll wear it for the second half.'

'I'll wear it for one hour and twenty-two minutes and you wear it for one hour and twenty-two minutes.'

'Right. Then we'll live next door to each other and our babies will be born on the same day and we'll push them around in one pram and nothing will separate us. Not ever.'

'Not even hurricanes or earthquakes or husbands who don't like each other.'

'We won't marry them if they don't like each other.'

Eleni nodded and yawned. 'Shall we all live in the same house?'

'Depends how rich we are. If we're really rich we can share one big house. I mean, they're going to be princes, aren't they?'

'Let's be really rich, then.'

'OK.'

And we drifted off to sleep. But it didn't work out like that.

Not the part about dreaming of our princes, because
that night I dreamt of being chased by a giant crab. But
not the other part, either. The part about never being
separated. That didn't work out at all.

It wasn't a hurricane, an earthquake or – euw –
husbands that did it.

It was me.

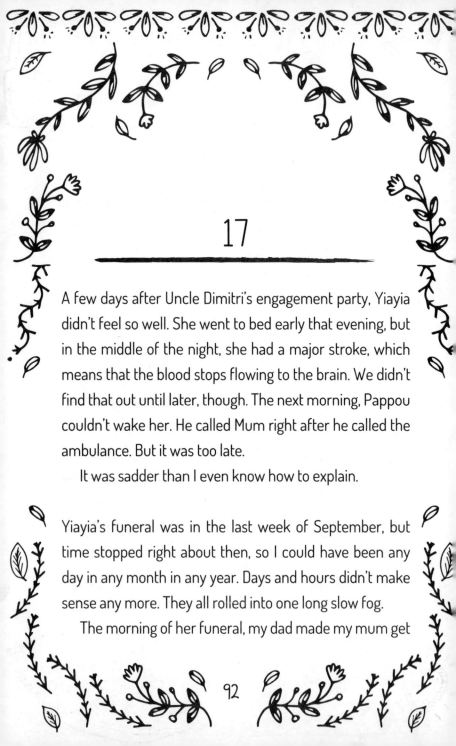

17

A few days after Uncle Dimitri's engagement party, Yiayia didn't feel so well. She went to bed early that evening, but in the middle of the night, she had a major stroke, which means that the blood stops flowing to the brain. We didn't find that out until later, though. The next morning, Pappou couldn't wake her. He called Mum right after he called the ambulance. But it was too late.

It was sadder than I even know how to explain.

Yiayia's funeral was in the last week of September, but time stopped right about then, so I could have been any day in any month in any year. Days and hours didn't make sense any more. They all rolled into one long slow fog.

The morning of her funeral, my dad made my mum get

dressed and put make-up on, even though she didn't feel like it. She was lying on their bed in the dark and Dad had to go in and physically pull her up.

'Your mother wouldn't want this. She'd want you to carry on as normal. And, anyway, what? You're going to look beautiful for every other special occasion and not for your own mother's? Tsshhh.'

So Mum forced herself to get dressed, and Aunt Soph came over and did her hair, but the air in the bedroom was flat and fusty, like the inside of a forgotten cupboard.

We buried Yiayia that afternoon and our world changed for ever.

A hundred people came to shake my Pappou's hand and kiss his wet cheeks. I'd never seen him cry before. I didn't even know he could. It made *me* cry because although I was sad, seeing *him* in pain was even harder. And seeing my mum, Aunt Soph, Uncle Dimitri and everyone else broken and in pieces was the worst thing ever.

It rained and rained and rained that day.

When we all went back to Pappou's house, Yiayia was missing from everywhere we looked.

*

93

Eleni and I lay on the spare bed to get away from all the people downstairs. We put our arms around each other like we were rocking on a boat on a choppy sea. Which I guess we were.

'Where do you think Yiayia is now?' I asked Eleni in a whisper. Because how could she be here and full of life one minute, and gone the next? Her glasses were on the sideboard. Her slippers were under her bed. Her favourite mug was in the cupboard and her fingerprints were on everything in the house. How could they still be here and she wasn't? It just didn't seem possible.

'The Greek part of heaven,' Eleni said. 'Eating *koulourakia.*'

'And meatballs. And *makaronia tou forno.* And making everyone else eat it too,' I added.

'And making sure all the ghost children do their home-work so they will have degrees and become doctors,' Eleni said.

I smiled, but a huge boulder sat inside my belly, making it hard to breathe. 'Do you think her ghost is still around?'

'If it is,' Eleni said, 'food will appear in the kitchen and we will have to eat it. And she'll make cupboards bang and

94

glasses fall off the shelves if we don't do our homework.'

That afternoon, we wrote letters to her in our notebooks, in case she could read them from heaven.

Dearest Yiayia,

We know you're around because we can feel
you so strongly but it's not the same, and
you need to come back now. Uncle Dimitri is
getting married and you're going to miss it.
We know you and God are close friends, so
please ask him if he will change his mind and
bring you back to us because we miss you so
much and everyone is a mess without you.

Love from Alexandra and Eleni xxxx

We waited for hours to see if a reply magically
appeared in our notebooks, but it didn't.

We went downstairs and everyone was staring at the
air and the floor in shock, like zombies. We sat there too

and joined in the staring, because we couldn't understand it, either.

I didn't think my heart could ever feel more hurt and broken than it did that day.

But there was worse to come.

I just didn't know it yet.

18

When people die, they're supposed to leave this thing called a will. It's a legal document that says who they want to leave their house, their money and their stuff to when they die.

Yiayia didn't write a will, which turned out to be the biggest mistake of the century. Because when it came to sharing out Yiayia's things, which everyone wanted, just to be close to her and remember her by, the trouble started.

About a week after she died, we sat around the table at Yiayia and Pappou's house. We were still in shock and missing her so much we could barely speak.

Mum was there, and my dad, and Aunt Sophia and Uncle Christos, and Uncle Dimitri and Christina, and my siblings and cousins. Pappou sat at the head of the table,

his head looking like weights were pulling it down and it took all his strength just to hold it up.

Eleni sat on my lap on a chair at the table. We held hands and linked legs and wondered if Yiayia's ghost was in the room with us because it sure felt like it.

They talked about some of Yiayia's things and who should have them, and we half listened and half looked around, trying to take in the fact that Yiayia had gone and she was never coming back to use them. The ornaments she'd collected sat on the shelves. Food she'd cooked was in the freezer. Photos of her smiled from the walls and the shelves, and if you looked closely, you could make out the dents where she sat on one side on the sofa.

After a while, Aunt Sophia, her brown hair tied back and her nails painted Toffee Ice Cream, cleared her throat and said, 'We need to talk about the wedding necklace.'

My eyes nearly popped out of my head. I think Eleni felt me turn stiff because she turned her head to look at me.

I knew this would come up at some stage, and I'd been dreading it. I'd kind of hoped they'd forgotten all about it. But no.

Mum looked at Aunt Sophia in confusion. Her hair was

neat and her make-up was perfect, but she looked flat, as if the life was leaking out of her in a slow hiss, like a punctured paddling pool.

'What . . . are you talking about?' she asked.

'The wedding necklace it go to Evangelina,' Pappou said, as if that was the only thing that made sense. 'She is the oldest girl.' Evangelina is my mother, but no one calls her Evangelina except Yiayia and Pappou. Everyone called her Ange or Angelina, or sometimes Lina-*mou*.

'But Dad,' Aunt Soph said, 'this is why we need to talk about it. I don't know how to tell you this, but . . .' She paused, looked at my mum, and then came out with it. 'Eleni said Mum wanted her to have the necklace.'

My mother froze. I did, too. I think the whole room did. Maybe the whole universe.

Mum whispered, 'What are you *talking* about?'

Aunt Soph took in all the eyes staring at her and carried on. 'She told Eleni about it just before she died. Obviously, Christina will wear it when she marries Dimitri, and when the time comes, Katerina and Kallie, and Elias and Nick's wives, and Lexie and Eleni. But Mum promised the necklace to Eleni when she was a baby.'

99

LIE!

There was silence. Every person at that table sat statue-still in shock. Everyone, that is, except Eleni and me, because we already knew.

'You what?' Uncle Dimitri asked. He was wearing a light shirt and had a long strand of Christina's dark hair sitting in an S shape on his arm. I wanted to lift it off, but it wasn't the right time. 'Where'd you get that from? I never heard Mum say that. Did you, Dad?'

'How could you?' Mum asked Aunt Soph in a tight, hard voice. 'What is it with you and taking my stuff all the time?'

'OH MY GOD! I'm not taking your stuff! This isn't about me. It's about Mum and the necklace.'

'That necklace is coming to me and you know it. It gets passed to the oldest girl. That's the tradition.'

'Do you think I don't know that? But it's not what Mum wanted. She told Eleni on the night of the engagement that she was keeping it for her.'

Mum's face turned white – she looked as if she was going to pass out. I'd never seen her like that before and it terrified me. Maybe I should have said something then but I couldn't. I was too afraid.

After a short silence that lasted forever, she looked at

100

Soph, shook her head and whispered, 'Unbelievable. How could you do this to me?'

'Angelina,' Aunt Soph said, leaning over to take Mum's hand, but Mum pulled it away like she'd just touched something red hot. Aunt Soph drew her hand back and said, 'Don't do this. I swear to you, this is what Mum wanted. She made this . . . deal with Eleni when she'd just come out of her first surgery. I know it sounds crazy but I'm not making this up. Eleni told me yesterday.'

Eleni's eyes fixed on me, but I couldn't look at her. The weight in the room made everything happen in slow motion and my whole body was stiff with fear. What should I do? What should I say? But actually, I couldn't do or say anything.

'Tradition,' Pappou said with a crack in his voice. 'Tradition says the necklace it go to Evangelina.'

'I know that, Dad. But, according to Eleni, Mum said herself that just this once her promise overrides tradition.'

'No!' Mum said, her eyes wild and angry as she stabbed her finger on the table. 'Nothing . . . overrides . . . tradition. I've loved that necklace since I was a little girl. I always knew it was coming to me. Don't take this away from me.

101

Not when I've lost her as well.'

Aunt Soph stuck her jaw out and said, 'You're not the only one who's lost her.'

'Girls!' Pappou shouted, making me jump. 'NO! Not this. Not this!'

Aunt Sophia gazed at Mum with pleading eyes, but Mum was staring at the air above the table with tears spilling down her cheeks.

'Ange, please. Listen to me. Why would I not want you to have it? I know how much you love that necklace. I just want to respect Mum's wishes. You *know* how she felt about Eleni.'

And then my mum snapped. With a fury face and spit spraying out of her mouth, she shouted, 'Eleni Eleni Eleni! Since the day since she was born all we ever hear is "Eleni"! What about *my* children? What about Katerina? She's supposed to get that necklace after me. What about Lexie? She's important as well, you know. Eleni is not the only child in this family!'

Aunt Soph gasped. I did, too. I'd never heard my mum say anything like that before. None of us had. We all knew how special Eleni was.

Pappou suddenly banged the table and shouted, 'NOT THIS! I SAY, *NO*! NOT THIS!'

My mother pushed her chair back hard, making a heart-scraping, brain-scraping noise. Her eyes were bright and furious and her nostrils were flaring. 'It's my necklace. End of discussion. Andy, get the kids. We're going.'

The rest of us looked at each other with frantic eyes.

'Course,' my dad said in his deep boom-bass voice, and picked up his new set of car keys. (The old ones never did work properly after being in the sea.)

I stood up and glanced at Eleni in panic.

Why didn't you say anything? she asked me in whale song.

But I couldn't answer. Not in words and not in whale song. Because I didn't even know myself.

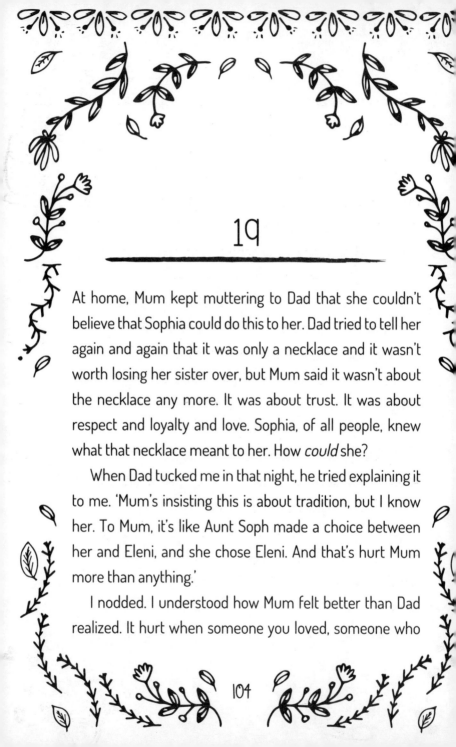

19

At home, Mum kept muttering to Dad that she couldn't believe that Sophia could do this to her. Dad tried to tell her again and again that it was only a necklace and it wasn't worth losing her sister over, but Mum said it wasn't about the necklace any more. It was about trust. It was about respect and loyalty and love. Sophia, of all people, knew what that necklace meant to her. How *could* she?

When Dad tucked me in that night, he tried explaining it to me. 'Mum's insisting this is about tradition, but I know her. To Mum, it's like Aunt Soph made a choice between her and Eleni, and she chose Eleni. And that's hurt Mum more than anything.'

I nodded. I understood how Mum felt better than Dad realized. It hurt when someone you loved, someone who was always there for you, acted in a way you just couldn't understand.

After that day, Mum went into a kind of haze. She couldn't eat or sleep, and because of that, she got sick with flu and ended up in bed. I don't like it when she's sick, but this was even worse because she wasn't just physically ill. It was like her mind had switched off and she'd turned into someone else completely. Even after she was well enough to get up, she refused to answer the phone or even look at her mobile. When she was alone, I'd catch her shaking her head in disbelief or groaning in her chair like she was in pain or going mad. My dad kept trying to talk to her about it, but she shook her head, and all she did all day was cry and cry and cry.

After a few days off school for the funeral and all our relatives coming over and everything, I had to go back in. I hadn't seen or spoken to Eleni since our mums had argued at Pappou's house, but when I saw her in the playground before the bell went, she wasn't cold or angry. I stood beside her without speaking but saying a thousand things in whale song, until she broke the awkward silence and

105

said, 'I've got a new pen.'

I swallowed, and in a nervous voice, asked, 'Oh yeah? What colour?'

'Red. Because red makes you write faster.'

We both smiled. When we were seven, we chose the same trainers, but hers were red and mine were blue. Elias told Eleni that hers were better because red made you run faster, which was obviously nonsense but she believed him.

Huh. Lies. Even then. I just didn't realize it at the time.

Eleni and I glanced at each other and she bit her lip. 'Why didn't you tell them?' she asked. 'What Yiayia said.'

I kicked at nothing on the playground floor. 'I couldn't,' I replied. And then I shrugged. 'My mum.'

Eleni nodded. Things were going to come between us that we hadn't even thought of, and this was one of them.

At break, we sat in the furthest corner of the playground and shared a banana. She took a bite. I took a bite. She took a bite. I took a bite. All the way down until the last speck was gone, and I said, 'greedy.' The shouty clangey noises of the playground echoed in the damp grey air. Kids skipped and ran past us. Others played football, shared snacks or argued. We were in our own private world. As usual.

I unfolded my white ankle socks and they came three-quarters of the way up my calves. Eleni was counting something, her finger bobbing every time she added another one. Sometimes it was people with red hair, sometimes the number of chimneys you could see without turning your head, sometimes the line markings on the tennis courts.

'I don't know what to do,' I said.

'Me neither,' she replied, her finger dropping on to her lap but her eyes still searching. Then her shoulders sagged, like she'd given up the count. 'Your mum should have it.'

'What about Yiayia's promise?'

Eleni blinked at me, like she does when she's about to say something blindingly obvious. 'Um. Yiayia's gone, Lex. She'll never know.'

I rolled my eyes. 'I do know that. But she made a deal. Probably with God. She said He talked to her all the time.'

Eleni paused. 'I wonder what God's voice sounds like. Do you think He's got a Greek accent?'

I considered that. 'Probably Spanish.'

She nodded. 'Or Australian. Like He goes up at the end of his sentences? You know? Like those girls in that mermaid programme?'

'I don't think God's Australian. They're laid back and go surfing all the time. God's not like that. Look what happens in the Bible. What if we break Yiayia's deal with Him, and He gets so angry, He destroys the world?'

She gasped. 'And it'd be all our fault.'

I swallowed. 'What's the right thing to do, Eleni?'

'Only God knows that,' she said matter-of-factly. She looked up at the sky, so I did, too. It was white with baggy grey clouds, like two-day-old mashed potato. I'd never thought of drawing the sky white. I always drew it blue. But it was white most of the time in England. Like it was waiting for someone to colour it in with felt-tips.

I couldn't see God up there, but then I wasn't sure what He looked like. And anyway, maybe the sky was actually the end of a giant telescope lens and He was watching us from far away. I waved just in case, and Eleni frowned and twisted her lips, but she did it, too.

'Hi God,' she said. And then she whispered, 'Do you think it's a bit rude to say "hi"? Maybe we should say "Good morning, Sir," or "Dearest Most Honourablest God in Heaven" or something, and not just call Him by his first name. I mean, we have to write 'He' with a capital H in

Greek school.'

She had a point. '*Is* God His first name?' I asked. 'Does He have a surname?'

She frowned. 'I didn't know the Queen had a surname until yesterday, so who knows? It's not like God needs one. Everyone knows who He is.'

'What's the Queen's surname?' I asked. 'Elizabeth . . .?'

'The Second.'

I burst out laughing. 'That's not her surname!'

Eleni squinted. 'Oh. Maybe it's Windsor, then. I wrote down "The Second" and "Windsor" but I wasn't sure which one it was. Isn't Windsor the place where her castle is?'

I grinned and nodded. I was still wondering about God's surname when Eleni added, 'I don't get it. If God talked to Yiayia, why doesn't He talk to us too?'

'I wish He'd tell us what to do,' I murmured.

'Let's ask Him.' Eleni wiped her hand on her shirt, looked at the mashed-potato sky and said in a loud clear voice, 'Dearest Most Honourablest God in Heaven.' She whispered in my ear, 'Just in case.' Then she continued, 'Please tell us what to do about the family necklace. You can tell us in English but we understand Greek and whale

song, too. Thank you, love from Eleni Kyriacou and Lexie Efthimiou, aged nearly eleven.'

'I think he knows how old we are.'

'In case He forgot. He has a lot of people to deal with.'

I nodded. She took my hand and we sat listening as hard as we could, staring at the sky for ages and ages, until the bell went.

God didn't answer. Not in any language that we knew of, anyway. So we had to go inside.

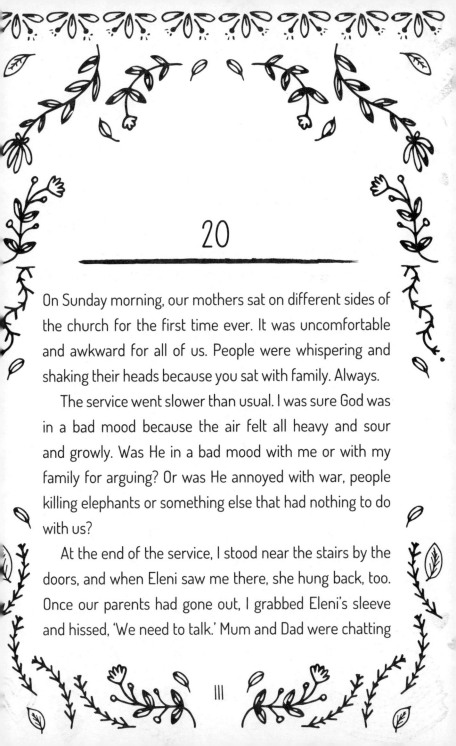

20

On Sunday morning, our mothers sat on different sides of the church for the first time ever. It was uncomfortable and awkward for all of us. People were whispering and shaking their heads because you sat with family. Always.

The service went slower than usual. I was sure God was in a bad mood because the air felt all heavy and sour and growly. Was He in a bad mood with me or with my family for arguing? Or was He annoyed with war, people killing elephants or something else that had nothing to do with us?

At the end of the service, I stood near the stairs by the doors, and when Eleni saw me there, she hung back, too. Once our parents had gone out, I grabbed Eleni's sleeve and hissed, 'We need to talk.' Mum and Dad were chatting

to people outside and didn't see me standing with Eleni, which wasn't allowed now. Aunt Soph and Uncle C were outside too, with Kallie and Elias, speaking to Father George.

'Let's go to the toilets,' I said. 'Come on, this is crucially vital.'

Just then Anastasia walked over. 'Sorry about your Yiayia,' she said to both of us with a sad smile.

Eleni and I stood there in silence. Not because it was a hard thing to hear (even though it was) but because no one had told us what to reply when someone says that to you. Are you supposed to say, 'It's OK,' (because it's not OK – not at all) or 'Thank you,' (which sounds wrong because thank you is for presents) or 'Yes, I'm sorry about that too,' which is obvious?

'My brother Pani's here,' Anastasia said. 'The one who plays for Chelsea Youth. Want to meet him?'

We knew about Pani. Playing for the Chelsea youth team was WOW, but still. That's not what you say straight after mentioning my Yiayia's death. It's just not. I was confused and needed God and Eleni to tell me what to do.

'Not now. We have a family emergency,' I said.

112

But Eleni said, 'Oh, **whoa**, he's *here*? I want to meet him! Come on, Lex. He's *famous*!'

'Eleni, we need to—'

Eleni glared at me with her big bushbaby eyes. 'You didn't say anything at Pappou's, so now they think *I'm* lying and my mum is, too. So unless you're going to tell them the truth, we don't need to talk about this *right now this second*. Let's go and meet Pani.'

She started to walk away with Anastasia and turned around when I didn't follow.

What? she asked me in whale song. And with her mouth she said, 'It'll only take fifty-six seconds. We can talk after that. Come.'

'I need the toilet,' I said, even though I didn't. Which was a lie I said **in church**, so it's probably worse than any other type of lie. Unless you lie *to a priest* in church, I guess.

'So come after,' she said. 'But come.'

And she walked away with Anastasia.

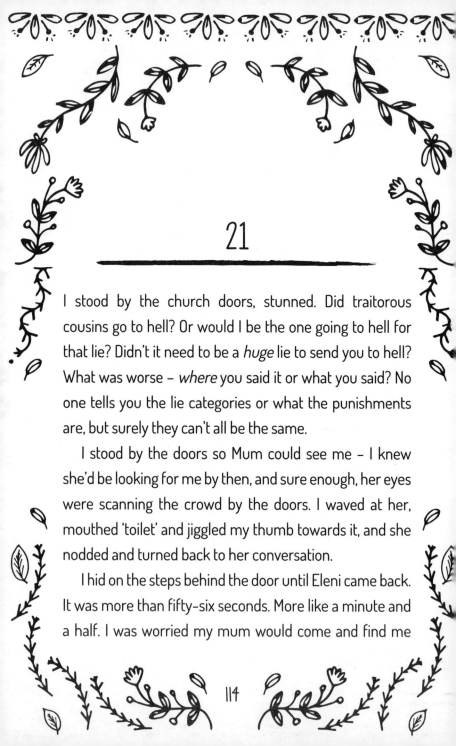

21

I stood by the church doors, stunned. Did traitorous cousins go to hell? Or would I be the one going to hell for that lie? Didn't it need to be a *huge* lie to send you to hell? What was worse – *where* you said it or what you said? No one tells you the lie categories or what the punishments are, but surely they can't all be the same.

I stood by the doors so Mum could see me – I knew she'd be looking for me by then, and sure enough, her eyes were scanning the crowd by the doors. I waved at her, mouthed 'toilet' and jiggled my thumb towards it, and she nodded and turned back to her conversation.

I hid on the steps behind the door until Eleni came back. It was more than fifty-six seconds. More like a minute and a half. I was worried my mum would come and find me and that would be that. But she was still outside talking.

'Why didn't you come?' Eleni asked in a hard voice when she arrived beside me.

I pulled her on to the steps. I was still annoyed by what she'd just said to me in front of Anastasia. 'Because who cares about stupid footballers?'

'I do, actually.'

'Oh yeah? More than sorting out our problem?'

'Obviously not, but it can wait one minute.'

'No, it can't. We might only have this one minute to talk, and you ran off. That's not very respectful, is it? Not to Yiayia's spirit or God's mood or our serious family crisis.'

'I didn't run off! I went to meet Pani. Why do you get so moody every time Anastasia's around? She's my friend as well, you know. '

All the hairs in my body stood on end. *Friend as well?*

As if Anastasia and I were . . . what . . . *equals?* I wasn't just Eleni's friend! I was *her cousin.* I was her *twin!*

I've never passed out, but I swear I nearly did it then.

I got up and walked away like I'd just been knocked out,

with Eleni saying to my back, 'I can do what I like, Lexie. You're not my ruler.'

I screwed up my fists and she must have seen me do it because she yelled, 'He's a *footballer!*' Which annoyed me even more.

I stomped over to my mum who was talking to someone about Yiayia. My eyes were stinging with tears and I was furious. How could Eleni say that? This wasn't about Anastasia, even though she was *nnngggghhh*, or even about football. This was about keeping our family together, and family meant everything to us. Well, to me, anyhow. And it was about our unbreakable bond – which, on second thoughts, wasn't quite as unbreakable as I'd thought.

After church, Pappou summoned us all to his house. We hadn't been there together since they talked about the necklace and the will. They sat Eleni and me down at the table. I didn't even look at her – I stared at a spot on the table and scowled.

Mum was by the fridge with her arms folded, definitely not talking to Aunt Soph. Aunt Soph was near the table, definitely not talking to Mum.

But Aunt Soph definitely wanted to talk to us.

She pulled up a chair with a hellish screech. She's shorter and thinner than my mum and she dyes her hair brick red, but otherwise they look the same. She leant so close, I could see the tiny holes in the skin at the side of her nose. Her hazel eyes were serious and blinky and tough.

'Girls,' she said in a Prime Minister voice. 'When did Yiayia tell you she wanted Eleni to have the necklace?'

Eleni tensed up. Even though we'd had an argument, her hand moved automatically to the side to take mine but I kept my hands firmly on my lap.

'It was after . . . Uncle Dimitri's engagement party,' Eleni said in a quiet voice. She peeked a look at me but I kept my hands down, clamped together, so she drew hers back towards her slowly, and I was glad she was hurt.

'Go on,' Aunt Soph said.

'She . . . um . . .' Eleni sounded terrified. 'She let us see it. Just for thirty-seven seconds . . . and that's when she told us.'

'What did she tell you, Eleni?'

'That when I was a baby she wanted me to stay alive so she . . . made a deal with me. And with God.'

'What kind of deal?'

'That if I was a good girl and didn't die, she'd give me the necklace. And because I didn't die, she said a promise is a promise, and she was going to give it to me.'

Aunt Soph leant back and took a deep breath. Then she turned and with her jaw jutting out, she looked at Pappou and my mother. 'You see?' she said coldly. 'I'm not making it up.'

The clock ticked, but the pause between each second felt like a century. Everyone in the room was silent. The boiler turned on and off again, like Yiayia was trying to say something, but I didn't understand what it was because I don't speak boiler language.

'Lexie,' my mother breathed. She was pale and had dark purple shadows under her eyes, and her hair had gone a bit frizzy. She looked kind of crazy, as if someone had flicked a switch in her head and turned Normal Mum off and someone else on. I didn't like it. 'Lexie, is that true?'

I knew I had to say yes or nod or something, but I was too scared. It was as if the earth was cracking in two with Mum on one side and Eleni on the other and I had to

118

choose who to jump to. If I said yes, Mum wouldn't be able to take it, and I didn't want to hurt her any more than she was hurting already.

But if I said no? I thought of what Eleni had just said to me and my back turned to prickles. *Friend as well? You're not my ruler?* Huh.

So I whispered, 'I never heard Yiayia say that.'

Silence.

The fullest, loudest silence I've ever, ever heard.

I could feel Eleni's eyes drilling holes in me but I stared straight ahead. Pappou coughed into his knuckles but didn't speak, and I wasn't sure what he meant by that. Dad's eyes were on me, and Pappou's, Uncle C's, Aunt Soph's, Mum's, God's, all the angels', the icons', and somewhere up there, Yiayia's. And right beside me, Eleni's. Eleni who said things that hurt me so much, I could barely breathe. Eleni who didn't think of me the way I thought of her.

Aunt Soph gripped the table with her hands until her knuckles went white. 'Wait,' she said, shaking her head. 'Wait.' She leant forward, frowning. 'You didn't hear it, or Yiayia didn't say it?'

LIE!

119

They were all staring at me and somehow, I felt stronger, so I said, 'I didn't hear her say that.' Deliberately and clearly.

Mum gasped. Bodies shifted in chairs, feet shuffled and Dad and Uncle C muttered something to each other in low voices.

Under the table, Eleni's small, pale hand tugged on the hem of my T-shirt and she whispered, 'What are you *doing*...?'

I looked at her with victorious eyes, but all around me I could feel the sky unhinging.

'Knew it,' my mother said through tightly-touching teeth. 'Unbelievable. Just unbelievable.'

Creeeeaaaak went the sky.

'But . . . but you were there when Yiayia said it!' Aunt Soph spluttered. 'Eleni, she was there, right? Lexie, just tell your mum what Yiayia said that night—'

'Enough,' my dad barked. He held out his big bear hands and lifted me to my feet. 'Enough. You've got your answer. Lexie, go with Mum. I'll get the others. We're going.'

In whale song, Eleni said, *You* did *hear Yiayia say that. Why are you saying you didn't?*

Because, I replied firmly, in whale song, *I can do what I like. You're not my ruler. And anyway, you were the one who told me to lie.*

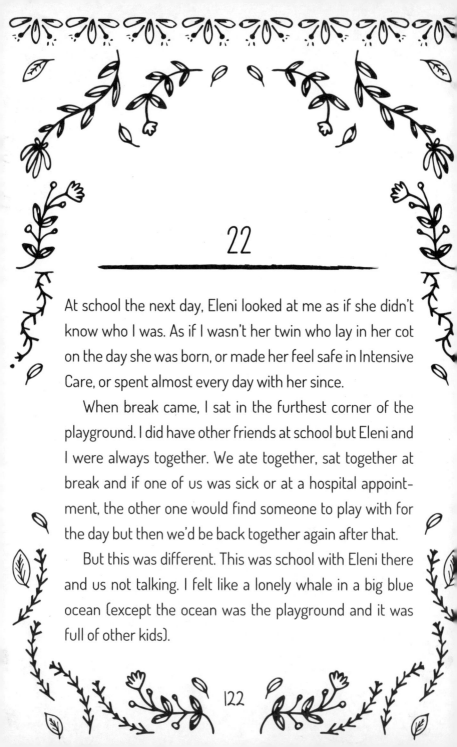

22

At school the next day, Eleni looked at me as if she didn't know who I was. As if I wasn't her twin who lay in her cot on the day she was born, or made her feel safe in Intensive Care, or spent almost every day with her since.

When break came, I sat in the furthest corner of the playground. I did have other friends at school but Eleni and I were always together. We ate together, sat together at break and if one of us was sick or at a hospital appointment, the other one would find someone to play with for the day but then we'd be back together again after that.

But this was different. This was school with Eleni there and us not talking. I felt like a lonely whale in a big blue ocean (except the ocean was the playground and it was full of other kids).

It was worse than the worst kind of horrible. Was tomorrow going to be the same? And the day after? And every day until I left to do a degree in dictionary writing?

That night, Katerina, Nicos and I were at Pappou's house. My parents were out and Pappou was asleep in his armchair with a low dark cloud of sadness sitting around him. Nick and Kat were watching something on Kat's laptop, so I crept into the forbidden *saloni*, sat on the sofa and gazed around numbly at all Yiayia's most precious things, which made my bones ache as if I was ninety-eight years old.

What would Yiayia have wanted me to do? Why didn't she whisper down from heaven and tell me? If she'd seen how broken Mum was, would she have wanted the necklace to go to her after all? Or would she have wanted Mum to accept that Yiayia had promised it to Eleni?

I sat there for five centuries, thinking.

After a while, I hauled myself up. Even though the crucifixes were glaring at me from the walls and the Virgin Maria kept telling me not to, I tiptoed upstairs to my grandparent's bedroom, closed the door and slid open the third

123

drawer from the bottom.

I slipped my hand in the drawer and felt under the clothes at the back. With my ears on high alert for someone coming and my heart walloping like an eagle in a cage, I drew out the small dark blue cloth. I opened it up and gazed at the necklace. Love for Yiayia flooded into me and tears spilt down my cheeks. It was so hard to believe that she was gone. And it was even harder to believe that a little Greek cross on a shiny gold chain could cause this much pain and misery.

I lifted my face to the ceiling and mumbled, 'Help me.' To God, or Yiayia. Not to the ceiling.

But there was only silence.

At least at first.

Then, suddenly, the solution became clear. I knew what God and Yiayia wanted me to do. If no one had the necklace, the problem would be solved.

I let out a long shaky breath and wiped my eyes. I folded the necklace in its blue cloth case, slipped it under my sweatshirt and quietly closed the drawer. Then I tiptoed back to the spare room, hid it at the bottom of my bag and put all my clothes on top.

I zipped my bag and went downstairs with my heart still walloping.

No one had even noticed I was missing.

When we went home, the necklace was deep in my bag, wrapped in my pyjamas. When Kat was in the shower, I took it out, covered the cloth case in sheets of her lined homework paper and then taped it all up. Then I placed it at the bottom of the shoebox in my wardrobe that I kept my old birthday cards in, put the cards on top, then the spare duvet back on top of that, and closed the wardrobe doors.

If no one knew about this except me, it was as if the necklace didn't exist and never had.

Our mothers would get over it.

Eleni would forgive me.

And we'd all be fine again.

Except it wasn't that easy.

23

A few days later, Pappou summoned us to his house.

My parents walked in with heavy shoes, edgy eyes and grunty coughs. Eleni's family was already there and the room was as welcoming as stinging nettles. Idols judged us silently from the walls and the Virgin had a holy frown. Yiayia was strongly and invisibly all around us, and she was not happy with the way things were going with her daughters.

Uncle Christos asked Nick and Kat to sit in the sitting room with Elias and Kallie, and the adults sat Eleni and me at the table. No one else. Just us.

Eleni didn't look at me, and I didn't look at her. We hadn't been talking in school lately, but now the necklace was gone, that was all going to change.

K

Aunt Sophia was still wearing black, like Mum, and it made their faces seem even more pale and washed out. Aunt Soph's eyes without make-up were small, and her red hair was tied back in a messy bun. She didn't look very lovely, and I didn't want to say, *I'm not her* in my mind because it wasn't very nice – she was my auntie, after all. She rested her hands on the back of a chair and her nail polish colour was Yesterday's Moussaka. My mother stood at the other end of the table, near Pappou. Her nails didn't have polish on, because she couldn't exactly ask Aunt Soph to paint them when she wasn't talking to her.

Daggers and fury breath filled the air where the aroma of *avgolemono* was supposed to be.

'Girls,' Pappou began. 'My heart it is heavy heavy.' And then, to prove it, he paused for a hundred and seven years and phooed a long sigh. 'We go to the place where Eleni tell us where is it – and the necklace it is gone.'

I swallowed.

'So we must ask you both of you.' Pappou's big hands were out in front of him on the table like he was holding himself or maybe the table steady. 'Do you know where is it the necklace?'

127

I sat still and said nothing. What if they knew? If they did, I was in the biggest trouble of my entire life.

Mum's arms were crossed and her nostrils were flaring. Aunt Sophia, with her chin jutting out, stared at us impatiently. Dad and Uncle Christos had their hands in their pockets and stood in awkward, uncomfortable hunches.

Aunt Soph said in a scratchy voice, 'We've turned the whole room upside down. The necklace isn't there. And it definitely was. So we need to know who took it.'

'Girls,' Pappou said, focusing his tired brown eyes on us. 'This is very verrry important. You must please tell us the truth. Did you take the wedding necklace?'

My brain jangled in my skull. I didn't know whether lying or telling the truth was the right thing to do any more, and this was *exactly* the time when I needed to know that. I glanced at the statue of the Virgin, and at the picture of Jesus on the crucifix and I wanted so much to be good and holy. But then I thought of how horrible this all was and how much I wanted it to be over.

'No, Pappou,' Eleni said in a soft voice, like drops of rain hitting an umbrella.

128

And then their bodies and their eyes and their hopes and fears and their anger and pain turned to me. I wanted to tell them what I'd done, I really did. But even more than that, I just wanted there to be no necklace at all and for our family to be back to normal again.

So, in a tiny voice, I said, 'No.'

Aunt Sophia threw her arms in the air and yelled, 'Knew it. Why would you even think the girls took it? Why don't you just admit it, Ange. *You* took it because tradition is more important to you what your own mother wanted!'

Mum gasped. 'You complete and utter—'

'Angelina!' my dad barked. 'Don't!'

'I told you, I didn't take it,' Mum spat in fury. 'You know I didn't. It's so obvious that *you* did, so why don't you just stop with all the pretending?'

'Girls, go!' Pappou said, waving at us, so Eleni and I scuttled out of the room.

In the sitting room, Eleni sat on one sofa and I sat on the other. Eleni didn't know the truth about the necklace and I wasn't about to tell her. Yes, I lied to Mum and Soph about Yiayia's deal with Eleni, and yes, Eleni was angry with me

129

and I was angry with her. But the wall between us seemed even higher now that our mothers were going for each other like two vicious animals in the kitchen.

'Flush,' Nick said. He and Elias were playing cards but you could tell they were tense – their shoulders were hunched up.

'Keep going,' Kat said to Kallie. She'd been scrolling on her phone but she kept looking at the door anxiously. 'They'll stop in a minute,' Kat added, but she didn't seem so sure.

Dad and Uncle C must have been freaked out too, because they arrived in the sitting room not long after us. Dad sat next to me and Uncle Christos sat next to Eleni and we all stared ahead, feeling numb. 'Put Channel 4 on,' Dad said, and Elias changed the channel. We all stared at the Grand Prix on the screen like life wasn't collapsing in ruins in the next room.

Duh da da dah dahdahdah, went the arguing in the kitchen.

Formula One cars roared across the track like giant car-shaped vacuum cleaners.

The arguing in the kitchen became more like *DA DA*

DAHDAHDAH DAH DAH DAH DAH DAH DAH.

Suddenly the kitchen door slammed. Dad and I looked at each other and our eyes said, *Uh-oh*.

Mum stormed in with a scarlet fury face. Tears smeared her cheeks and she looked scary.

'Get your coats on,' she hissed through white rigid lips.

'I'm about to win—' Nicos protested.

'I SAID GET YOUR COATS ON!'

24

Mum and Aunt Sophia refused to talk to each other after that.

They kept searching Pappou's house but the necklace wasn't found. Of course it wasn't – it was in a shoebox in my wardrobe. Every day, a thousand hundred times a day, I thought about telling them where it was, but I was even more scared than I was before. I'd get in so much trouble now. They'd go mad at me for taking it, but they'd go even madder when they found out I'd lied to their faces and caused this terrible war.

Soon enough, they'd forget about it, I told myself. Christmas would come, Easter would come, we'd get together to laugh and eat, and the necklace would be forgotten. Maybe they'd even laugh about it one day.

Maybe.

A couple of days later, I casually asked my mother what she'd do if the necklace turned up. Just to see what she said. Maybe if I confessed now, it would all blow over.

'It's not about the necklace any more,' Mum said in an icy tone. 'You don't do that. Not to your sister. I don't want anything to do with her. That's it.'

Everyone tried to make peace between Aunt Soph and my mum, but nothing worked.

'What will we do at Uncle D's wedding?' I asked, even though it wasn't until next summer.

'You'll stay right next to me,' Mum said coldly. 'And don't sit with her at Greek school either.'

I didn't like to tell her that wasn't even an option any more. Eleni sat with Anastasia at Greek school now.

That Sunday, Dad watched football alone. Nicos and Kat moped about the house, being grumpier than usual, and that's saying something because teenagers are grumpy all the time. They frowned a lot, mumbled one-word answers and stomped up the stairs, which was normal, but that day they did it with the volume turned up.

Mum was in her room and I went in to see if she was OK. After Yiayia died, Mum kept Yiayia's dressing gown, which she didn't ever wear, but I caught her with her face buried in it, sobbing so deeply her whole body was heaving. I thought she was trying to suffocate herself in it, so I watched, terrified. My mum had turned into someone I didn't know and now she was trying to kill herself with a dressing gown.

When she realized I was there, her giant sobs slowed into gulps. It stopped sounding as if she was desperate for oxygen and more like she had bad indigestion. She wiped her eyes on her sleeve, held out the dressing gown and said, 'Smell.'

Even though I thought she was being super weird and scary, I smelt the dressing gown and Yiayia flooded over me in a giant wave. The sudden memory of her made my eyes sting. It smelt warm and safe and kind. I bit my lip because it started wobbling but I couldn't stop my face from crumpling. Mum nodded, her eyes puffy and her nose running.

'I know,' she said. 'Say goodbye. I'm putting it back.'

I wanted to but I couldn't. Say goodbye to what? The smell? The dressing gown? It wasn't to *Yiayia* because she wasn't there. Mum wrapped it up and returned it to the top shelf of her wardrobe. She blew her nose on some toilet paper she had by her bed, threw the roll to me, and once I'd blown mine, she came over and pulled me towards her for a hug that went on for ages.

That night in bed, I thought about how weird it was that people's smells stay in the world when they've gone. I wonder if Yiayia's smell will eventually fade from her dressing gown or whether it'll still be there in a hundred years. Maybe the world is full of the smells of people who aren't here anymore and we just don't know it. Maybe that's what makes us feel sad for no apparent reason sometimes, I don't know.

All over half term, I was bored bored bored. I usually spent every holiday with Eleni but that was before. I wrote in my notebook most of that week because I had nothing else to do and the only person I could talk to was a piece of paper. Which is not even a person.

135

> Hello, piece of paper.
>
> Hello, Lexie.
>
> How are you, piece of paper?
>
> I'm flat and white, thank you. How are you?
>
> I'm bored out of my head and talking to my notebook, which is just sad.
>
> I'll cheer you up. Did you know that the Sami people have a specific word for a reindeer whose 'hair near its nostrils is of a different colour from what one would expect in view of the colour of the rest of its hair'?
>
> Lovely Notebook, that would have made me happy once, but now I don't even care.

The first day back after the October half term, Eleni didn't show up to school. She hadn't told me she wasn't coming – not with her mouth and not in whale song, either.

But when she didn't appear, the teacher announced that she'd moved to the school on the other side of town. The one Anastasia went to.

Everyone spun around to look at me, gasping and whispering. I felt bare and open, like my insides were on view for all to see. Despite twenty-seven other kids being in the room, I had never been more alone.

When I went to sit in the playground that break, the circle of space around me felt as deep and wide as the universe.

I pretended I didn't care and everything was fine, but my heart was the one that needed surgery now.

137

PART
2

Six months later

25

It was the first Wednesday in February and the world felt like a giant freezer. The week before, snow had fallen like giant puffs of frozen fluff but Uncle D had cleared the path, so all that was left were small, grimy icebergs lining the edge of Pappou's drive. If you stood to one side and squinted, they looked like a mini mountain range topped with grey and black peaks.

When we were little, Eleni and used to stomp on snow clumps because we thought our footprints made new ice lands that we were the queens of. I breathed a long hiss of dragonbreath into the icy air, and tried not to think of her, but sometimes you can't make your brain do what you want it to do. With the wind biting my face, I jumped on a snow clump with my boot, crushing it into a hard mash of ice. *Cruunnnch*. And there it was. Lexie-land. A brand-new country. All mine.

'Lexie!' Mum honked. 'What're you doing? Take this – it's freezing.' She handed me an orange carrier bag from the boot, closed it hard and headed up the path. She was doing better now. She was grumpier than she used to be, and more serious, but at least she was up and doing stuff. It was the right decision not to tell her about the necklace. Wasn't it?

Steaming breath was rising from her nostrils like her head was boiling and her brain was evaporating into the chilly air. I raised my boot and stomp-stomp-stomped, making three more Lexie-lands, and then ran up the drive behind her.

Pappou opened the door looking scruffy and crumpled, like a used paper bag, just with white hairs sprouting from his chin. His face was saggy and grey, and his clothes looked like he'd slept in them.

We'd dropped Nick and Kat off earlier, and I'd gone with Mum to get Pappou a prescription (which he calls a 'description' because he mixes the words up). Mum had bought him tea and other bits because, you know, the snow, even though only three centimetres had fallen and he already had enough food in his house to last for fifty years.

Pappou grunted and shuffled along the corridor. Before Yiayia died, he would open the door and roar 'Hellooooo' so loudly that the neighbours at the end of his road could hear it. Then he'd hug us one by one, kiss us on both cheeks, and take us out to show us whatever it is he was proud of in his garden that day. Sometimes a fat courgette. Sometimes a mini lemon on his young lemon tree.

Mum frowned and followed Pappou inside. I slunk in behind her with my eyes glued to the floor so I wouldn't see the photos covering the walls in the hallway. There was one of Mum, Soph and Dimitri with weird haircuts, smiling in their 1970s school uniforms. One of the whole family at Aunt Soph's wedding, lined up in rows in our fancy dresses and three-piece suits. And one of Yiayia and Pappou at Mum and Dad's wedding, with Soph in the background, her eyes full of tears because she was so happy for my mum on her wedding day.

I couldn't look. Those photos made my skin itch and my belly lurch.

It hadn't got to the point yet when we walked through Pappou's door and it felt normal that Yiayia wasn't there. As I walked past the sitting room on my way into the kitchen, Nicos called me.

'Whatssup?' he said when I stood at the sitting room door and peered at him. He was watching TV but he looked bored.

I shrugged and he eyed me suspiciously. 'Feeling all right, likkle sis?'

Nicos talks like that because he's fourteen and thinks he's some bad-boy gangster even though he's a nice Greek boy from South London. He wears his trousers hanging down like he's lost a ton of weight or his belt or both, which makes him shuffle when he walks like he has a big full nappy. It looks the opposite of cool if you ask me.

'As if you care,' I muttered.

'Course I care. If you're not feeling good, you can't get me any cookies, can you?'

I turned and marched off.

'LEX! Get me cookies! PLEEEEASE! YOU'LL BE MY FAVOURITE SISTER!'

I ignored him and went into the kitchen.

144

Pappou was at the sideboard turning down the radio. He listens to LGR (London Greek Radio), which is always crackly.

'What's wrong, Dad?' Mum asked as she placed the shopping bags on the counter. She had no make-up on and her face looked like the sky in winter, or a ghost. Which I didn't want to think about. She watched Pappou like a detective, but she must have been a bad one who couldn't find any clues because she asked, 'You OK?'

'Euh,' Pappou said, sitting heavily in his chair. Pappou's armchair has buttons to make the back lie flat and the foot rest go up. It's so cool but we're not allowed to sit on it and pretend we're at the dentist or piloting a spaceship. Nick and Elias played on his old chair a few years back and broke it so this one was a no-grandchildren zone.

'What does "euh" mean, Dad? Maybe you can give me a bit more detail?'

'Euh.'

'Ohh-kay,' Mum said, not taking her eyes off him. 'Let me put this stuff away and I'll come and talk to you. Did you eat? Got some *stifado* and *souvlaki* for you.'

He nodded. Kind of. More of a head flick.

'Good. You need to eat, Dad. Lexie, come.'

I didn't want to but I sat down at the table – the one covered in the giant doily – and Mum fixed me a pita stuffed with *souvlaki* and salad, even though I'd rather have had spaghetti with halloumi. I peeked a look at Pappou because he wasn't himself and it was scaring me. He was rubbing his forehead and staring at the wall.

'Pappou?' I asked. 'You OK?'

He lifted his arm and waved it like he was sending a servant out of the room. I knew what that arm wave meant. It meant, 'euh'. Poor Pappou. I understood him. Of course he felt 'euh'.

He wasn't the only one, either.

146

26

I picked up my pita, took a small bite and chewed it slowly.

In my notebook I'd been writing down all the stuff Yiayia used when she was alive – stuff no one paid any attention to – that now glowed with spooky energy.

- Her face cream is still on her dressing table, ready to be used, but her face isn't around any more to put it on.
- Her clothes are in the wardrobe.
- Her mug is in the cupboard next to her tea.
- Her glasses wah-wahed at me yesterday, I swear.

Everywhere you looked, there she was. Except she wasn't. We were desperate and aching to see her again, but we never would. Now she only existed in our minds, like we'd made her up. I just couldn't get my head around that. And poor Pappou had to live there with all those constant reminders.

I stared at Yiayia's rings. They were sitting in a little hand-painted saucer from Cyprus. I wanted to add them to my list but I didn't have my notebook with me. So I sat chewing and thinking.

My plan hadn't worked at all.

I thought that with the necklace gone, everything would return to normal. But six months had gone by and Mum and Aunt Sophia still weren't talking. Which meant we weren't talking to any of their family and they weren't talking to any of ours. We stood by Mum, and they stood by Aunt Soph, I guess. We didn't go in and out of each other's houses with smiles, hugs and pots of food. We didn't sit next to Aunt Soph's family in church – we sat on the other side and looked everywhere but in their direction. At the stained glass. At the people kissing the feet of icons and sweeping their hands across the floor. At the constant

candle-lighting commotion. At the priest clink-clinking the smoking incense-holder on its chain. Not at them. I repeat. Not at them.

And we didn't go to Pappou's for lunch after church on Sundays, which was weird because we'd been doing that every week since I was born. Now Mum took us on Friday night instead so we wouldn't see *them* there. And Mum phoned Pappou every time she wanted to go around to make sure we wouldn't bump into them.

We still saw them around the neighbourhood, obviously, because they only lived a few roads away and we all lived in the same small community. But we avoided each other. Mum crossed the road if she saw them up ahead. Two days before, she'd put her shopping basket – full of stuff – at the end of an aisle and walked out when she saw Aunt Sophia and Kallie by the fridges in the supermarket. It was so awkward. I didn't know where to look. I went bright red and tripped over my feet on the way out. And I didn't get my Tic Tacs. Not that was the worst thing about walking out of there. Not by a long shot.

The world might have seemed like an OK place from the outside, but what felt warm and full and complete now

felt cold and empty and broken. Or maybe that was just me. Except I knew it wasn't just me. Everyone felt it. Not just my parents and siblings but all our cousins, aunts, uncles and distant relatives as well. Probably the whole Greek community. Maybe even the entire world.

As I chewed, the icons looked down at me from the walls. Yiayia was very religious. When I was young, I thought Yiayia was holy and if I touched her, it was like touching God. I was convinced that if I did anything naughty, like draw on the wall with Mum's lipstick (which wasn't naughty because I ruined the wall but because I ruined the lipstick), all I had to do was touch Yiayia's hand and this glowing light of forgiveness would wash over me.

Apart from Mary and baby Jesus, I wasn't sure who the icons were but they all had haloes and very thin noses. Most of them glowed gold, either from around their heads or from their faces, like they had a radioactive tan, but not one of them was smiling. Being holy must be a serious job. I mean, the whole truth lie thing is complicated enough, never mind having to save the world and everyone's soul. And if you're turned into a picture on the wall of Greek houses, you have to constantly watch them eating yummy

150

food and you can't have any. No wonder they weren't smiling.

Mind you, no one was. Not today.

Kat and Nick had eaten already – I could see their plates in the sink. I was still trying to eat my pita but how could I when I was being judged by the nameless holy people?

'And the wedding?' Pappou asked in Greek. He said it out of the blue in a thundery voice. He brought it up every time we went to visit but it wasn't like we were in the middle of a conversation right then or anything.

Uncle Dimitri's wedding was originally going to be in July, but they'd decided to bring it forward to the date of Yiayia and Pappou's wedding. Dad said they'd done it for Yiayia, to keep her memory alive, and as a sign of love and respect. Except Yiayia and Pappou got married at the end of February. Which was in three weeks' time. So now we had a problem.

Changing the date was a sweet thing to do but what kind of wedding would it be with Uncle Dimitri's family not talking to each other?

I took another bite and chewed slowly. I'd had enough, but Mum kept looking at me with *just-eat-it-will-you* eyes

so I forced myself to keep going. At least I could eavesdrop on their conversation, which I usually liked. But this time, I wasn't sure I wanted to. Because Pappou was right.

What were we going to do about the wedding?

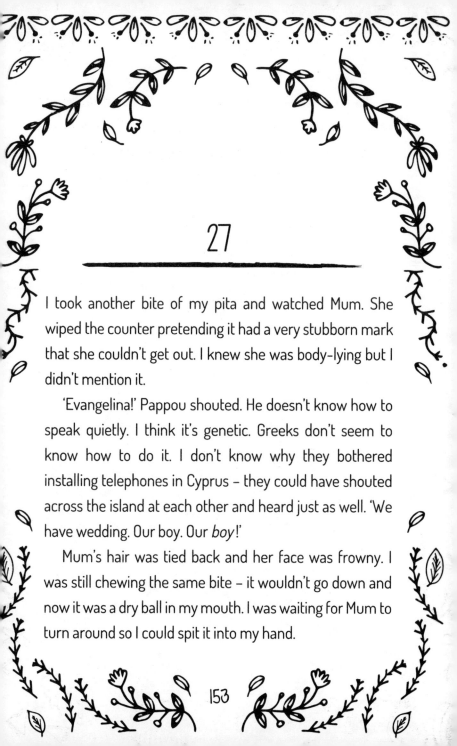

27

I took another bite of my pita and watched Mum. She wiped the counter pretending it had a very stubborn mark that she couldn't get out. I knew she was body-lying but I didn't mention it.

'Evangelina!' Pappou shouted. He doesn't know how to speak quietly. I think it's genetic. Greeks don't seem to know how to do it. I don't know why they bothered installing telephones in Cyprus – they could have shouted across the island at each other and heard just as well. 'We have wedding. Our boy. Our *boy*!'

Mum's hair was tied back and her face was frowny. I was still chewing the same bite – it wouldn't go down and now it was a dry ball in my mouth. I was waiting for Mum to turn around so I could spit it into my hand.

'We'll work it out,' Mum said, pulling the tea out of the shopping bags.

'How? How we work it out?' Pappou barked from his chair.

'They can get married twice,' Mum suggested. '*She* can go to the first one and we'll go to the second one.'

You should have seen Pappou's face.

'Marrrrrriiiiied? Twiiiiice?' he cried. 'They need make **two times** wedding because you won't stand in same room as your sister?'

Mum gave a half smile. 'OK. Maybe not.'

'Of **course** not! So?' Pappou's hands were flying about now. Greeks have hand gestures for pretty much every situation, including *Are you seriously suggesting having two weddings?* Surprisingly.

'What we do?' Pappou yelled. 'What we do about you brother wedding?'

'I dunno, Dad,' Mum snapped. She turned to put the tea in the cupboard, so I quickly spat the mouthful out and closed my fingers around it. It felt gross. Squishy and dry at the same time. 'Haven't really thought about it, have I?' Mum muttered.

Well, that wasn't true. Course she'd thought about it. She might not have had a solution but she'd thought about it for sure. She was getting edgy as well, because she couldn't find an inch of space for the tea and instead of just putting it in the garage like she usually did with the extras, she was tutting and moving things about.

'Two weddings?!' Pappou cried in Greek and banged his hand on the armrest in frustration. 'What *craziness* you speak!'

I put my pita down and sat there with the ball of gunk in my hand. I was hoping Mum wouldn't notice it and make me put it in my mouth again.

Mum said, 'We'll work something out, Dad,' and tucked a strand of hair behind her ear. I swear, Mum could lie so easily.

Which made me think.

So what if we lied? What difference did it make if we told the truth or told bare-faced lies every single day until we died? There were probably Vikings or Romans or Egyptians that spent their whole lives lying, and thousands of years later, no one knew and no one cared. Everyone told lies. Everyone. Except maybe priests and nuns but even they probably did at least *once* in their lives. I'd have asked Father George about it but it's not the kind of thing you feel comfortable asking a priest.

And nothing happened if you lied, either. Mum didn't get punished for it by being struck down with lightning right there and then, which was just as well because that would have been a bit *whoa*. God didn't care either. He didn't give liars and criminals nasty diseases or let my dad win the lottery, even though he bought a ticket every week. It was all completely random. The world would spin like a blue and green disco ball hanging in the universe and life would carry on either way. What was the point of even *trying* to tell the truth?

'Can't eat any more,' I said, pushing the plate away. The pita was soggy, the insides had turned into a chickeny mush and I still had the globule in my hand.

'Eat!'

'If you make me, I'll puke *souvlaki* all over the floor.' It was a lie but so what? I liked the idea of spending my whole life lying. I could make up all kinds of wild stories about myself.

*

Yeah, hi. I'm Lulu Balulu McCheesecake O'Reilly. I'm thirteen and a member of the Spanish Royal family. I have ten albino hamsters, a cat called Fatso Catso and a giant tortoise called Fluffy that transports me from my palace to my school on the back of its shell.

'Tut. What's the matter with you – it's tiny!' Mum shouted, still stuck on the pita problem and pointing at it with her hand. When Mum shouts, it's not bad or mean– she just talks like that.

I shrugged. 'Not hungry.'

Lie. I was actually quite hungry. I just didn't feel like eating when Pappou was so miserable.

Mum marched over, pulled me towards her and felt my forehead. 'You're not even sick!' She sounded disappointed.

'Do you want me to be?' I asked.

She gasped. '*Banayamu*. What crazy nonsense do you get in your head?' Then she shrieked and put her hand on

157

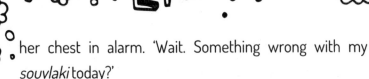

her chest in alarm. 'Wait. Something wrong with my *souvlaki* today?'

I rolled my eyes. She's so weird.

'Who will be *kumbarous*?' Pappou shouted from his armchair. *He* was still stuck on the wedding.

The *kumbarous* are like the best man but lots of them. They stand with the groom like his personal army of best friends. They're not just *kumbarous* for the wedding day, either. They stay your *kumbarous* for ever, like close friends for life. Two of Uncle Dimitri's *kumbarous* were Dad and Uncle Christos, but now they weren't talking to each other. And with Yiayia gone and my mum and Aunt Soph not talking either, this was going to be the most awkward wedding in history.

'You girls are killing me,' Pappou muttered.

'Oh my *God*!' Mum stared at him and then at me with bulging eyes. 'Dad, it'll be fine!' she said. Lying lying lying. 'Stop with the "killing me" stuff, will you? It's doing my head in.'

'*Keeellling* me!'

Mum grunted. Loudly. More like a roar.

'Fine. You know what? I love you very much, Dad, but

158

I'm going home. I can't talk about the wedding right now.'
Then she screeched, 'Kat! Nick! We're going!' and in a
quieter voice but you could still have heard her in the very
north of the country, she said, 'Get your shoes on, Lex.'

I still hadn't thrown the glob of dry food away yet.
Luckily I managed to drop it in Pappou's bin when Mum
was in the toilet or I'd still be holding it now.

28

Pappou sat in his chair with his shoulders slumped. What could I do? There had to be a solution. Apart from, you know, the obvious one that would get me in massive trouble and make everyone hate me.

'*Entaksi*, go, go,' he muttered gruffly as we said good-bye. 'Call later check if I still alive after you keeeel me with your two weddings.'

I gulped. Was that supposed to be funny? Because it wasn't. I was really worried about death now. It could happen to anyone I knew at any time. I could come home from school and Mum could be gone, or Dad, or Pappou. Or, most likely of all, Eleni.

'Please stay alive, Dad,' Mum said as we headed to the door. 'I've just bought you more tea.'

Wait – was *that* supposed to be funny? I laughed out loud for a long time in case they were all joking, but I don't think they were because they both looked at me strangely and Mum felt my head again.

None of this was funny at all. It was tragic. It had to end. How could Uncle Dimitri get married with the family like this?

In the car, Mum turned on the ignition and stared at Pappou's door. She was worried. About him. About the wedding. I knew she was – she just hid it well. Which means you can lie with your behaviour, not just your mouth, and that's a whole different level of lying.

'Two weddings?' I muttered as we pulled out of the drive.

'Came to me on the spot. Got any better ideas?'

I decided to be brave. 'I dunno ... you could ... maybe ... talk to Aunt Soph?'

Mum sniffed, lifted her head and tutted. 'Not happening. Any *good* ideas, I mean'

'That's the only one I've got.'

'Looks like it'll be two weddings, then,' Mum said. I knew she didn't mean it. She was lying but jokey-sarcastic-lying,

which is also a thing if you think about it. All the way home, I stared out of the window, imagining being a liar for the rest of my life. I could start this evening.

Even though we were in the car and my handwriting looks like a five-year-old who's had too much sugar when I write in the car, I scribbled down:

Lies:

- Say I've had a shower when I haven't had one since last week.
- Laugh my head off at one of Dad's three-out-of-ten jokes.
- Put small stones under my pillow and pretend they're teeth to get money.
- Say I have no homework when I have a sheet of maths and two pages of *Private Peaceful* to read.
- Say we've learnt about the history of doughnuts in school when we've really learnt about the water cycle.

When we walked through the door of our house the air was dull and flat and stale as a month-old mouldy pancake. The Efthimiou family might have been carrying on as usual but our house was full of missing. Not that anyone talked about it. Not to each other, anyway. It sat like a mist in every room. We all hid what we felt behind it and acted as if we were completely fine. But we weren't.

Mum drifted into the kitchen. It has white tiles and a white counter, but the cupboard doors are pale blue, and we have a pale blue kettle and toaster to match. It looks like a Greek church under an early-morning Cyprus sky, except it has a dishwasher and a sink.

Mum clicked the kettle on and then stood still, like a malfunctioned robot or a toy that had run out of batteries. She acted so well when we were out, no one noticed she was in a bad way. She could have got an Oscar for her chats in church, her smiles at school, her cheeriness in the street with the neighbours. But at home, the acting stopped. She walked around our house like she was lost. She picked up photos of Yiayia from the shelves and started quietly crying. I caught her doing it a few times and she wiped her eyes and said she'd been cutting onions.

163

Which was a lie. But I was getting used to that. Who even told the truth, anyway?

What Mum needed was Aunt Soph. Not that she'd *ever* have admitted it.

I turned around to go upstairs. I hated seeing Mum like this. On my way past, I stuck my head in the sitting room. Dad was watching football – we'd heard it from the hall when we came in – but I still wanted to see him. Just, you know, to make sure he was still alive and everything. It wasn't a Crystal Palace game – it was some European Cup match: I could tell because the players had names like Schmuckerhafen, Blumquistenburg and Kackerlack-alacka.

Dad was sitting on his armchair, eating peanuts. He'd have watched the match with Uncle C before all this and they'd be laughing their heads off and roaring at screen as if the players and the ref could hear them.

'Lexie-*moooou,*' he said, spotting me and popping another peanut in his mouth. 'You OK?'

I nodded but stayed half hidden behind the door.

'Pappou good?' he asked.

I nodded again. Which was a lie, but I didn't feel like

going into it and lies seemed just as good as anything else.

'Is the door acting like an invisible force shield stopping you from coming in?'

Two-out-of-ten Dad joke. Not funny. I shook my head.

'Tongue snatchers snip off your tongue with their snappy shears?'

I frowned and shook my head, just in case he was asking me for real.

'Ooooo-kkkay then. Well, it's fascinating chatting to half of you from behind the door but can you please shush now? No, really. Your constant jibber jabber's hurting my ears.'

I looked at him blankly. What was he even talking about?

He did a belly laugh. 'Come over here, oh silent one, and give your dad a hug.'

I went over and he pulled me into his strong, hairy arms so all I could see was darkness and all I could smell was his Dad smell, which would stay in the world after he was gone. Which made tears spring to my eyes because I didn't want to think about that. Not ever.

'Jeez, you're getting thin, girl,' he said, not letting go. I didn't mind because I didn't want him to see my eyes welling up. 'And from a Greek home, too. Tsssh. Your mother'll be so ashamed. They'll think we don't feed you. Or worse, they'll think or her cooking is bad. Huuuuuhhhh!' he let go of me and clapped his hands over his mouth in horror. 'Better go and eat something before you shame the family. And get me some juice while you're at it,' he added with a wink. When you're the youngest everyone uses you as the butler. I was used to it. I nodded and blinked to bat the tears away.

'You all right, Lex?' he asked, concerned.

I nodded again. I don't know why I didn't feel like talking but I just didn't. He was joking around like nothing was wrong but he was sad too, which meant *he* was good at lying with his body as well.

He reached out to me but I turned away and walked to the kitchen to get him some juice. As I took it out of the fridge, I thought about Dad. He pretended he didn't miss Uncle C but I knew he did. Uncle C made Dad laugh like no one else – don't ask me why. *The Six O'Clock News* is funnier than Uncle Christos.

I took a tall glass out of the cupboard and the carton of

apple juice out of the fridge, and went in to give them to Dad. He took them and looked at me for a longer-than-normal time. 'Where's Mum?' he asked, eventually.

I didn't feel like speaking but I had to use actual words now because unless I waved and pointed my arms, it seemed a bit stupid not to tell him. 'Sitting at the table.'

'She all right?'

I paused. Should I lie and say she was fine? I could have but there didn't seem much point. He knew the answer already anyway. 'Not really.'

He nodded slowly, then he did a long blowy sigh. He turned off the match, saying, 'Who cares if it isn't me old Palace, eh?' Then he went in to see Mum with his juice in his hand.

I stood in the hall for a while, looking at a photo of my mum smiling at her fortieth birthday party, then I followed him in.

 167

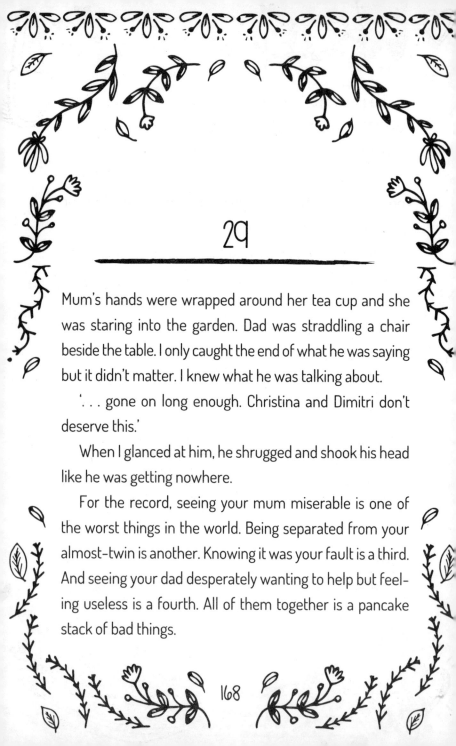

29

Mum's hands were wrapped around her tea cup and she was staring into the garden. Dad was straddling a chair beside the table. I only caught the end of what he was saying but it didn't matter. I knew what he was talking about.

'. . . gone on long enough. Christina and Dimitri don't deserve this.'

When I glanced at him, he shrugged and shook his head like he was getting nowhere.

For the record, seeing your mum miserable is one of the worst things in the world. Being separated from your almost-twin is another. Knowing it was your fault is a third. And seeing your dad desperately wanting to help but feeling useless is a fourth. All of them together is a pancake stack of bad things.

The phone rang. I was closest to it, so I answered it. I heard Mum mutter, 'Whoever it is, I'm not in.'

'Hello?'

'Hi Katerina,' a woman said, not giving me time to correct her. 'It's Biatra Hadjipateras. Can I speak to your mum, please?'

Lots of people had tried to talk sense into Mum since Yiayia died. They'd probably tried it with Aunt Soph as well. I don't know about Aunt Soph but Mum wasn't budging.

'She not in,' I said. Lying *because I was told to by my own mother*. Which is all kinds of wrong.

'Honey, I know she is. Tell her it's me.'

I went into the kitchen with the phone and held it out to Mum.

'I told you – I'm not in!' Mum mouthed at me.

I held the phone to my ear. 'Mum said she's not in.'

Biatra laughed. 'Put me on loudspeaker so she can hear me.'

So I did.

'I know you're there,' Biatra said to the whole kitchen but mainly to my mum. 'Lina-*mou*, enough. She's your sister. Your *sister*. More important than a necklace. You

169

hear me? Your *sister.*'

'It's not about the necklace any more,' Mum said, suddenly deciding she was in. 'Even if she gave it back tomorrow – and I know she's got it – it wouldn't make the slightest bit of difference. She's not my sister. Not any more.'

I put the phone down, I went into the sitting room and took out my notebook.

In the quietest times, when it was just me inside my head and no noise – you know, when you go to that place deep inside you where the truth is supposed to be (if the truth really was a thing) – I asked myself this: what was the point getting in a truckload of trouble when it wouldn't fix anything anyway?

Still. I couldn't handle Mum being like this any more.

So I wrote:

I want:
• to see Mum and Soph laughing.

- to watch them painting each other's nails Congealed Pig Blood, Highly Polished Coffee Table and all the other weird colours they have in their collection.
- them to plan *Paska* (Easter) together and figure out how to make Pappou interested in fat courgettes and mini lemons again.
- them to hug and cry and help each other deal with the fact that Yiayia's gone.
- this to be over and for us all to be a family again.

I put my pen down and wiped my eyes. Dimitri and Christina deserved an extra special wedding with Dimitri's sisters smiling beside him, and the day was coming towards us like a high-speed train. It was sad enough that Yiayia wasn't going to be there. Getting married like this was going to be horrible.

And as for marriages, how were Eleni and I going to marry two brothers on the same day and have a big fat Greek wedding with puffy dresses, tables full of

loukomades and bags of *koufeta* if we weren't talking and neither were our families?

I closed my notebook and climbed the stairs.

Nicos was in his room. I don't go in there. It's a no-go zone. Not because he tells me to keep away or anything, but because, you know. Teenage boy. Thinks he's cool. Really isn't. Nicos has weird uneven hair that's shaved short at the sides and long on top, like the barber ran off half way through the haircut. And, don't ask me why, but he gets away with everything because he's a boy.

His door was half open. I could see him on his bed, holding up one of his hideous new trainers. He'd designed them online. They were neon yellow, orange and blue with green stars on them, and they were seriously yuk.

'Look at my new trainers, Lex. Sick, aren't they?' he said when he saw me.

I nodded and I wasn't even lying: they really did look like vomit.

'No one's got trainers like these. They're one hundred per cent unique.' Nicos might have said 'no one' but he meant Elias.

'That's great,' I replied, and I truly meant it. The world did not need more trainers like those in it. 'Maybe you could, you know, phone Elias. To tell him. He'll like them, for sure.' Meaning, *apart from you, he's the only person in the entire universe who will like them.*

Nicos looked up. '*What?* No!' he said with a frown.

'Why not? Don't you want to make him jealous?' Nick and Elias were massive rivals. They were best friends but they still argued about everything. Now Nick didn't have Elias to compete with about everything from Frisbee throwing to gaming, he was a bit lost.

'Because,' he said. 'I'm not going against Mum.'

'But if one of us starts talking to one of them, it might get Mum and Soph talking. And then Mum would be happy again.'

'I'm not going behind her back. And neither are you.'

'But I miss her,' I murmured.

'She's downstairs. Go say hi.'

'Not Mum,' I said, rolling my eyes.

Nicos grinned, and then twisted his lips to one side. 'Stand firm, sis. This isn't about you. This is important to Mum. And she needs to know that we've got her back. OK?'

I made a face, walked off into my bedroom and sat down on my bed.

Every time I went in there, the necklace screamed at me from inside my wardrobe like something from a horror film. Even if it had been at the bottom of a thousand blankets and a million wardrobes, I would still have felt it. It was like the story about the princess with the pea under her mattress (but a scary version of the story with an evil pea that I'd created myself). I'd been so paranoid that Mum would find it, but no one looked in the shoebox with my old birthday cards in it, not even her.

I didn't want to think about what would happen if she did.

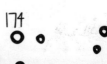

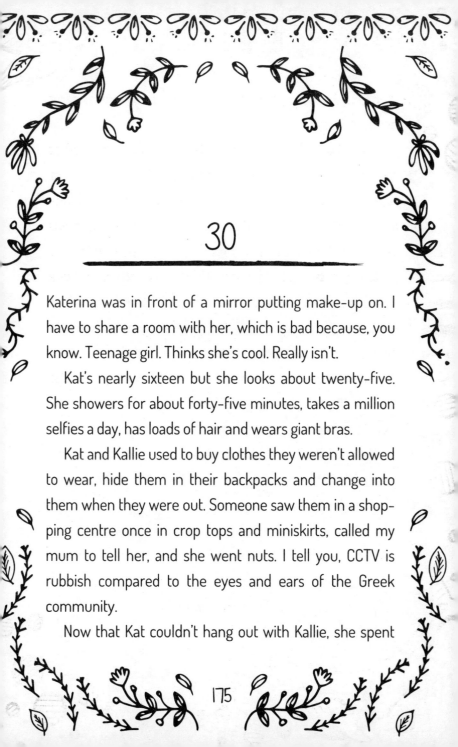

30

Katerina was in front of a mirror putting make-up on. I have to share a room with her, which is bad because, you know. Teenage girl. Thinks she's cool. Really isn't.

Kat's nearly sixteen but she looks about twenty-five. She showers for about forty-five minutes, takes a million selfies a day, has loads of hair and wears giant bras.

Kat and Kallie used to buy clothes they weren't allowed to wear, hide them in their backpacks and change into them when they were out. Someone saw them in a shopping centre once in crop tops and miniskirts, called my mum to tell her, and she went nuts. I tell you, CCTV is rubbish compared to the eyes and ears of the Greek community.

Now that Kat couldn't hang out with Kallie, she spent

her time experimenting with make-up. She was getting good at it, too. Each time she came out of our room she looked different. And beautiful, even though I wouldn't tell *her* that. The downside was that she was always late for school because she spent twenty minutes every morning doing her eyebrows. They're thick and dark anyway, and after she does whatever it is she does to them, they look like they have personalities of their own, and are ready to leave her face and start living in a flat somewhere with their friends. Mum doesn't know that's why Kat's always late – she thinks she just takes ages to get dressed. But I know the truth.

I didn't care about my eyebrows, and they were happy living at home.

'I don't get the whole eyebrow thing,' I said as she combed hers with a weird wand. 'Why is that even a thing? They're just hairs above your eyes.'

'Course they're not just hairs above your eyes.'

'Umm . . . duh. Yes they are.'

'Tut. What do you know? Let me do yours. They look like caterpillars crawling across your forehead.'

'Wow, thanks.'

176

She laughed.

'No way. You can show me how to do that flicky line, though,' I said. 'Up here,' and I ran my finger over my upper eyelid.

'Takes ages to get right. I'll show you when you're like fifteen or something. You'll waste all my eyeliner.'

I groaned and lay on my bed. The necklace screamed at me but I put my hands over my ears and hummed 'All Things Bright and Beautiful' so I wouldn't hear it.

'Don't you miss Kallie?' I asked Katerina mid-hum. We'd never spoken about it, which was crazy. No one in my house ever mentioned it. It freaked me out because it was always there, right in the middle of everything, and everyone pretended it wasn't.

Kat fixed her eyes on me for a few seconds and then ran her tongue over her front teeth. 'Course,' she said after a pause. 'But Soph shouldn't have done that to Mum.'

'Yeah, but you and Kallie could still be fri—'

'D'you know what loyalty is, Lex?'

I nodded.

Kat turned back to her eyebrows and said, 'Good.'

I sat up with my eyes scorching. 'Where was the loyalty

LIE!

177

at the picnic? Huh? When you all turned against me?'

Kat swung around. 'You snitched, Lex – you can't do that. We *were* loyal to you—'

'No, you weren't.'

She thought about that for a second. 'Fine, you're right. We weren't. Because you snitched and that's not on. But this is different. Course I miss Kallie, and I know you miss Eleni, and maybe it's stupid to argue over a necklace but it meant a lot to Mum and now she's hurt like she's never been hurt before, and she needs us. OK?'

I threw myself back on my bed and stared at the ceiling. This was all my fault. I'd ruined everyone's lives.

I'd ruined mine as well, of course. I didn't feel OK for ages after our families split. For the first couple of weeks, the smallest things made me cry: someone being mean, the toothpaste falling off my brush into the sink, not being able to untie the laces properly in my shoes. Stupid stuff. After three months, I only cried when I was going to sleep, which was a big improvement. But knowing I'd made them suffer as well was terrible.

I placed my hands over my eyes and curled up in the smallest part of myself.

Eleeeeeniiiiiii, I called in whale song. *I neeeeeeeed yoooooooouuuu.*

But the echoes of her answers were getting harder and harder to hear.

I saw Eleni around, of course. For a start, I saw her in Greek school every week, which made my stomach lurch like I was going down too fast in a lift.

Most days, she walked straight across the classroom, right in front of my table, and sat next to Anastasia. They chatted and laughed and I tried not to overhear. One week Eleni wore the same purple ankle boots as Anastasia. They both had plaits woven in a circle around the backs of their heads and I know Anastasia's mum had done them because I overheard.

Sometimes I felt Eleni looking at me across the classroom but I didn't look back. I caught Anastasia looking at me sometimes as well. I kept my eyes down and refused to give them the satisfaction. It was bad enough missing Eleni. I didn't need to feel jealous as well.

And I did miss her. But I was annoyed with her, too. I switched from missing her to being annoyed with her

179

about ten times a day. I don't know if that's normal but I didn't even know what normal was any more.

	8 a.m.	10 a.m.	12 p.m.	2 p.m.	4 p.m.	6 p.m.	8 p.m.	10 p.m.	To-morrow	Next week	Rest of my life
Annoyed with Eleni		✓		✓	✓		✓				
Missing Eleni	✓		✓		✓	✓	✓	✓	✓	✓	✓

180

HAHA HA HA HA!

31

That Sunday, I walked up to Greek class thinking of what I could do to fix the mess. The wedding was so soon. Time was running out.

There were only six other kids in the classroom because I was early and most of them stay out playing until the very last minute. I sat where I usually sit and after two minutes, Demi came in and said, 'Hey.' I must have been looking pretty terrible because she added, 'You OK?'

I nodded. Lying. She sat beside me and said, 'What is it?'

Now, Demi loves drama. She lights up when trouble starts, and she talks about people behind their backs, so you just *know* she talks about you to other people, too. I looked out of the window with my stomach lolling like a boat on stormy waves. I didn't want to talk to her because I didn't trust her, but I also didn't want to keep it all bottled in. She pulled my sleeve and led me out to the corridor where it was private.

'So?' she asked, standing at the top of the furthest staircase and offering me a crisp. 'What's wrong?'

'Nothing,' I lied.

'Lexie,' Demi said, licking her salt-and-vinegar fingers, 'If it's about Eleni being stuck like glue to Anastasia, don't worry about it. Everyone thinks they're ugh and annoying. They live in their own little world and they ignore everyone else.'

I kept my eyes down. If she was trying to make me feel better, it wasn't working. Eleni wasn't ugh and annoying. I wanted to stand up for her but at the same time, I couldn't because they really did stick together and ignore everyone else. Did Eleni and I used to do that? Probably. I hadn't thought of it like that.

But I didn't want to talk about them. Not to Demi, and especially not when I had to try and patch things up before the wedding. So I pretended I'd just remembered something. 'I didn't finish that homework. Did you? It was so hard and she's going to ask us for it now.'

182

Demi talked to me about homework for a few minutes and just before class started, I went to the toilet, leaving Demi in the classroom with Eleni and Anastasia. Which, looking back, wasn't a very clever thing to do.

I was heading back into the classroom when I heard Demi mention my name, and I froze outside the door.

'—what Lexie just told me,' Demi said.

My body became a leopard stalking a deer. Still. Hunched. Fully aware. My brain was screaming, *Oh yeah? What did Lexie just tell you?*

The next voice was Anastasia's. 'What do you mean? What did she say?'

My ears twitched. I moved my head slightly. *What was Demi doing?*

'She said you two were annoying and cliquey and you ignore everyone.'

My neck flesh fizzled and my feet fused to the floor.

'Lexie *said* that?' Eleni asked in a quiet voice.

'Yeah,' Demi lied. 'She said you don't know what it means to be a real friend.'

My eyes flashed wide open. That low-down traitorous... How **could** she?

I charged into the classroom and screeched, 'You *LIAR!*' Just as Kyria Maria walked in and yelled, 'What's going on in here?'

My skin was burning from my feet to my scalp. 'Nothing,' I muttered. Lying.

'Good, then sit down. All of you. Lexie, I'll see you at break. We've got a lot to do before then.'

I didn't move. I wanted to go home and never come back, but Mum wasn't picking me up for three whole hours. I wasn't allowed to walk home alone, and I couldn't exactly hide for that long in the toilet.

I could feel their eyes on me so I gritted my teeth, scraped the legs of the chair across the floor and sat down. Then I held my head high, even though my face felt hotter than the centre of the earth. For the rest of that lesson, Kyria Maria talked in Martian while my brain bubbled like a simmering pot of *stifado*. Next thing I knew, chairs were scraping and legs were scurrying past me for break.

'Lexie, I'll talk to you at the end of break,' Kyria Maria said. 'I need to move my car.'

I nodded and looked over to see Eleni and Anastasia's striding out of the classroom with Demi shuffling like a

K

little snivelling rat close behind. I glowered at her, my dark eyes glistening, but she slid past as quick as she could and scurried out the door.

I grabbed my coat off the back of my chair, stormed out of the classroom and marched downstairs. I didn't want to go anywhere near them but I couldn't stay in that class-room a second longer. Downstairs, the three of them turned left into the churchyard, so I stormed off to the right.

The world looked cruel and ugly. The wind scratched at my cheeks and the clouds brewed with dark mean thoughts. I sat hunched in the furthest end of the car park behind the bike shed where no one would see me, my breath deep and raggedy like I was Darth Vader with a cold. I'd never been so furious and humiliated in all my life.

I could see them from there. Anastasia had some stupid new ball – small and hard and green. They were playing tag with it near the front entrance. Eleni threw it, trying to hit Demi, but Eleni's throws are weak. I wanted to take it off her and throw it at Demi myself. Hard. Again and again and again. I narrowed my eyes but I couldn't stop glaring at them. I never knew lies could make you feel so angry.

 185

Eleni would never talk to me now. Even if our families *did* start talking to each other again. I needed to say something.

I got up and started walking towards them.

The next part happened so quickly.

Anastasia threw the ball. It shot past Demi and rolled to Eleni. Eleni picked it up and threw at Anastasia, but she missed. Anastasia ran after it, grabbed it, and threw it at Demi, but Demi stuck her foot out and the ball ricocheted off and smashed into a small window in the corner of the church. I heard a tinkling crash and saw shards of glass fall and speckle the ground.

I was still ten metres away but I was close enough to see their reactions. Demi's hands clapped over her mouth. She stared at Anastasia and Eleni in horror and all three of them glanced at me, ran to the main door and pegged it upstairs – they didn't even go and get the ball back.

I was the only one outside by that point. I looked around in alarm and ran towards the stairs too, just as Kyria Maria turned in from the main road and saw me standing beside the broken glass.

186

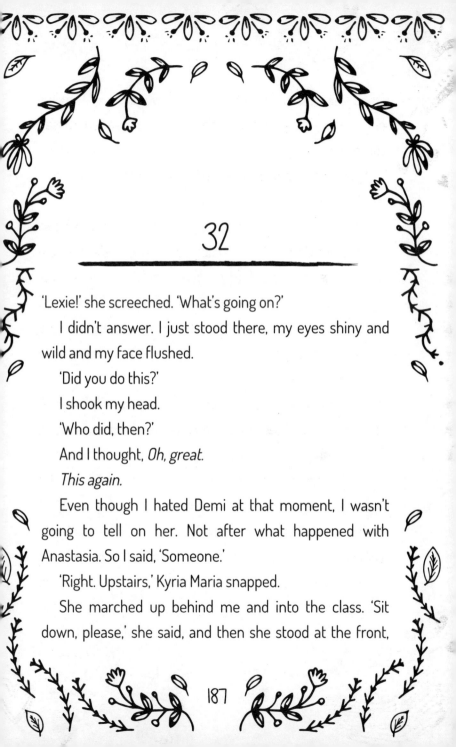

32

'Lexie!' she screeched. 'What's going on?'

I didn't answer. I just stood there, my eyes shiny and wild and my face flushed.

'Did you do this?'

I shook my head.

'Who did, then?'

And I thought, *Oh, great.*

This again.

Even though I hated Demi at that moment, I wasn't going to tell on her. Not after what happened with Anastasia. So I said, 'Someone.'

'Right. Upstairs,' Kyria Maria snapped.

She marched up behind me and into the class. 'Sit down, please,' she said, and then she stood at the front,

shook her long dark curls and folded her arms. Her arms are well muscly because she's into exercise and goes to the gym all the time (Mum told me) so you don't want to mess with her. She might be small and pretty but she could lift a bus in each hand.

'Someone has just smashed the small window downstairs. I'm going to ask you all just once who did it and I want an answer. So? Who was it?'

She looked at us and waited. No one said anything. Seconds went by that lasted a hundred years each.

'I see. In that case, I'm going to nominate someone to tell me.'

I swallowed. My face was so hot, so you could have fried eggs on my cheeks, but I kept my eyes on the desk and my mouth shut.

'Aredy, who broke the window?'

Aredy wriggled in her chair like her jeans were crawling with maggots and said, 'I don't know. I was upstairs the whole of break.'

'Demi? Did you see what happened?'

I squinted at the table. As if that lying toad would tell the truth. I didn't twist around to look but Demi must have

188

shaken her head because Kyria Maria moved on to me.

'Lexie? I'm coming back to you because you were the only one who was there. If it wasn't you, you're going to need to tell me right now who it was.'

You could have roasted potatoes in my stomach. Done a barbeque on my scalp. My lips welded together and all that came out of me were invisible funnels of rage.

'Well, then, we have a problem.' Kyria Maria's voice was cold as winter in Russia. 'If you can't tell the truth, Lexie, you'll have to stay behind so I can talk to your parents.'

I tried not to spontaneously combust but I was thinking, *Truth?*

TRUTH?
Do. Not. Even. Mention. That. Word.

The rest of the lesson, Kyria Maria was in a monstrous mood.

I sat there squirming. We were still in church, don't forget. Broken windows and lying weren't very holy. We were all going to go to hell, for sure, and that was freaking me out, but that still wasn't a good enough reason to tell Kyria Maria what had happened. I tell you something, trying to understand the whole truth–lies thing is more

hellish than any hell I could ever picture.

Kyria Maria kept me back after class, and when Mum arrived, she told her about the window. 'I have to assume it was Lexie,' she said. 'Seeing as no one's told me otherwise.'

'Did you break it, Lexie?' Mum asked, right there and then, in a voice so loud and hard, people in Denmark took cover under the table. Her eyes were filled with shock and shame and disappointment and all those bad things you don't want to ever see in your mother's eyes.

I frowned and stuck my jaw out. 'No.'

'Who did, then?'

'Not me.'

'If you can't say who it was, then you're guilty,' Mum said. Don't even ask me where she got that nonsense from. 'How *could* you? In *our church*! If Pappou knew...'

Pappou had been chairman of our church for about twenty years. He wasn't now but it made him a bit like the Pope in our community.

'Sorry, Angelina, but I'm going to have to ask you to pay for the window,' Kyria Maria said, putting her hand on Mum's arm.

'No, *course*. Send me the bill.'

'First I have to find the caretaker and ask him to cover it up so we don't get broken into.'

Mum gasped. 'Oh no. I didn't even think of that.'

'Meanwhile, perhaps Lexie here should reconsider her relationship with the truth.'

Invisible insects crawled around under my skin. I wanted to shout, *Yeah? Really? You think so?* but I was in enough trouble already.

Mum edged away from me like I was a violent criminal. She shook her head and said, 'I'm so sorry, Maria. I don't know what's got into her. It's probably . . . you know.'

Which annoyed me. *It's probably 'you know' what?*

Kyria Maria said, 'That's what I thought, too.' Which annoyed me even more.

Mum gave Kyria Maria a look and said, 'It's late. We've got to go. Say hi to your mum. Tell her the *tiropita* she made for Nikki's birthday was the best I've ever tasted.'

Kyria Maria said, 'Oh my God!' (which can't be a good thing to say in church, right?). 'She'll be over the moon! Bye, Angelina. See you at Zumba.'

33

When we got to the car, Mum turned into a giant barking dog. She woofed angrily at me at a hundred miles an hour about honesty being the most important thing in the universe *rurrurrurrurruh* and I should be the one paying for the window *woofwoofwoofwoofwoof* and what was I *thinking* and how did I break it anyway? With a rock?

'I didn't break it,' I yelled.

She stopped barking at me for a second. 'Well, who did then?'

'Someone else.'

'Oh yeah? Who? You were the only one there.'

I sat there with injustice fizzing and bubbling inside me like an unstable science experiment about to go

boom.

Five minutes later, when we turned into our road, Mum said, 'So listen to me, when you go into Greek school next week . . .' and that's when the lid came off.

I yelled, **'I'm never going back to Greek school ever in my entire life. I hate every single one of them in that stupid class and I hate Greek and most of all I hate you because you make me go when you know I hate it!'**

Mum slowed right down and stopped the car. Luckily, we were in our cul-de-sac by then and not on the main road. Still. She just stopped! In the middle of the road! Isn't that illegal or something? I wanted to ask but I was boiling, erupting and steaming at the time.

'Finished?' she asked, not looking at me.

'No, I have not finished!'

'So finish. Go ahead. I'll wait.'

But I couldn't because by then, I was snorting like a bull and trying not to cry.

Eventually, Mum said quietly but firmly, 'You're going

193

LIE!

next week. And the week after. And the week after that. And every week until you're sixteen. Just so you know.'

When I got home, I was the grumpiest I've ever been in my life. I slammed doors. I stomped around. I growled loudly at Dad's three-out-of-ten Dad jokes. Mum sent me to bed at 6 p.m. as a punishment for breaking the window, so I flung the toothpaste back on the side of the sink without closing the lid and brushed my teeth so hard, enamel must have rubbed off. Then I marched into my room, threw myself into bed and pulled the duvet over my head.

Being dramatic and angry was kind of fun. I felt like a teenager. But I got bored after ten minutes. 6 p.m. is *early*. So I got out my notebook and started writing. Not just fun stuff this time, but everything that happened, right from the beginning. And it felt good to get it out. For once, someone was listening to me. Even if that someone was a piece of paper in a book.

DON'T LIE!

194

LYING MANUAL

Have you ever been so close to someone that you could wah-wah in whale song?

I have. Well, sort of, anyway.

When I say 'wah-wah', I mean communicate, but not in a normal way. In a special telepathic way that wah-wahs out of your brain and into theirs, or wah-wahs out of their brain into yours.

About half an hour later, when I was lying in bed in a strop, the phone rang.

'Oh, hi Maria,' I heard Mum say, and then she muttered something quietly, which I didn't even realize she could physically do. I tried to eavesdrop but I needn't have bothered because Mum yelled, 'Lexie! Come.'

I didn't budge. Mum called twice more and then came upstairs. I pretended I hadn't heard, which, if you think  about it, is another type of lying. Mum held out the phone and said, 'Kyria Maria. She wants to talk to you.'

I stared ahead like Mum wasn't even standing there.

195

'Take the phone. Talk to your teacher.'

I shook my head.

'Lexie!'

But I wouldn't.

Mum put her hand over the mouthpiece and whispered to me, 'That is so rude. Don't you dare do that.'

I looked up and replied, 'Do what?' Which is lying through acting, if you think about it. Did that even count as lying? Actors did it every day.

'Talk to her.'

My brain turned into a stormy place. I snatched the phone and mumbled, 'Hello?'

'Lexie, I want to give you one more chance. Tell me the truth about the window.'

Poisoned purple pus burnt my insides. I wasn't going to answer but Mum was standing next to me with her arms folded, so I muttered, 'I didn't break it.'

'Then tell me who did.'

What are you supposed to say at times like these? What?

And then something in me snapped. I'd had enough. So I told her the truth. Kind of. In a firm voice, so they'd both

hear me loud and clear.

'I didn't break the window, OK? Someone else did. But I can't tell you who it was because that's called snitching. I have no idea why snitching is worse than being honest, but it is. So all I can tell you is that *I* didn't do it and that's the truth.'

I handed the phone back to Mum and threw the duvet over my head. I was quite pleased with myself, actually. I'd found a way to tell the truth without exactly telling the truth. It was brilliant.

Now all I had to do was figure out how to do the same thing with the necklace.

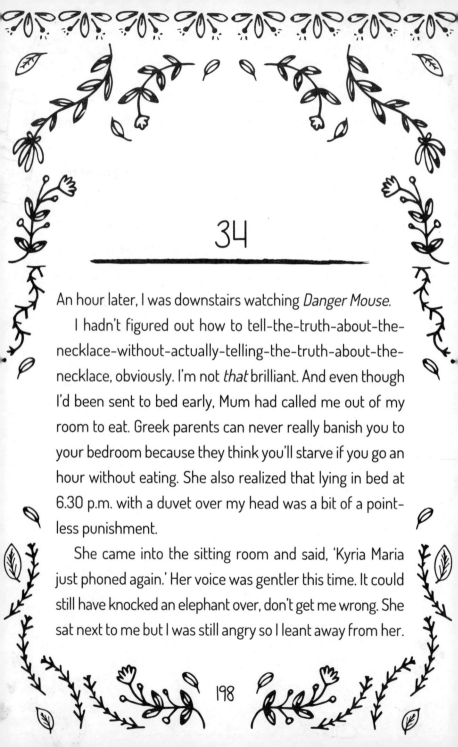

34

An hour later, I was downstairs watching *Danger Mouse*.

I hadn't figured out how to tell-the-truth-about-the-necklace-without-actually-telling-the-truth-about-the-necklace, obviously. I'm not *that* brilliant. And even though I'd been sent to bed early, Mum had called me out of my room to eat. Greek parents can never really banish you to your bedroom because they think you'll starve if you go an hour without eating. She also realized that lying in bed at 6.30 p.m. with a duvet over my head was a bit of a pointless punishment.

She came into the sitting room and said, 'Kyria Maria just phoned again.' Her voice was gentler this time. It could still have knocked an elephant over, don't get me wrong. She sat next to me but I was still angry so I leant away from her.

'She called a couple of your classmates after she talked to you. Someone told her who broke the window. She knows it wasn't you.'

I sucked on my teeth. She could have called any of the eighteen kids in our Greek class but if she only called 'a couple', one of them was sure to be Eleni. She must have told Kyria Maria I didn't break it. Huh. Nice to know she still stood up for me.

I kept my eyes on the TV. An advert came on about people living this perfect, happy life because they used the right washing powder. Which means adverts also lie. Lies, lies everywhere. You can't get away from them.

'Lex,' Mum said, putting down her *kanela* tea, 'if you knew who did it, why didn't you say?'

'Because!' I said, turning to Mum in a rage. 'Remember the car keys?'

Mum glared at me and held her finger up. 'I told you then and I'm telling you now. The best thing to do – always – is tell the truth.'

'That's not true, Mum,' I said.

'Course it is.'

'No, it isn't! What if telling the truth hurts someone?

Huh? Or you get someone in massive trouble and everyone hates you?'

Mum made a 'hmm' face. Luckily, she didn't get the hint about the truth hurting someone. It was a risky giveaway clue but she didn't seem to notice.

'I know what you're saying,' she said. 'But still. The truth is important.'

I glared at the TV. I wanted to say, *Like the truth that you miss Aunt Soph so much, it's breaking you in half? Like the fact that you cry all the time and won't admit it? Like pretending the wedding is going to be fine when we all know it isn't?* But I didn't because I knew saying any of those things would hurt her. Loads. And I didn't want to do that.

'Ange!' Dad called from the dining room. 'Phone! It's Dimitri.'

Mum didn't move. She just sat there rigid, like she was afraid.

'Mum,' I said, confused. 'Phone.'

'He wants to talk about the wedding,' Mum said in a flat robot voice. 'And I'm going to tell him we're not coming.'

'*What?*'

200

'He's not going to like it,' she added. And out she went.

I sat there, stunned.

We had to go to Dimitri's wedding. We *had* to. Did she *mean* that?

On TV, Danger Mouse was tied up in a building. A big round bomb lay right beside him with the fuse sizzling, about to go off. The words 'CRUMBS!' and 'CRIKEY!' flashed on the screen in yellow comic font.

It's about to explode, Danger Mouse! I shouted at him in whale song. *Better do something, quick!*

You can talk! Danger Mouse replied in whale song. Even though he's a mouse.

And he was right.

When I went into the kitchen, Mum was unloading the dishwasher with a crash and a smash. I'm surprised we have any plates left.

'Well?' I asked.

'He's not having it. He said we have to go.'

Relief flooded over me. *Course we have to go!*

'But I told him we're not and that's final,' Mum said, and she carried on trying to break all our dishes.

35

I went to bed (at nine, which is a normal aged-ten Greek Cypriot time for going to sleep, not 6 p.m., which is before babies even go to bed).

I couldn't sleep. I had to work on Mum. It was the only way. I needed to get her to talk to Aunt Soph again. The wedding was in two weeks and I was getting panicky. If we didn't go to Dimitri's wedding, it would arrive and pass by without them talking, and if that could happen, we could easily go through the rest of our lives without talking. Easters. Christmases. Birthdays. Summer barbeques. Our graduations. Our weddings. Maybe they wouldn't ever talk again, and the thought of that made me want to faint and collapse, even though I was already lying down.

I had to come up with something.

I reached to the side table for a pen, and opened my notebook.

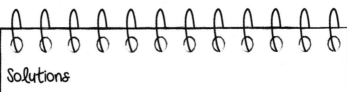

Solutions

1. Tell Mum Aunt Soph is sick?

X Don't like lying about sickness (for obvious reasons).

2. Get them to meet 'accidentally'?

X Mum walked out of the supermarket when she saw Aunt Soph

3. Tell them about. . .

X No way.

I put my pen down. I knew the third option was the only thing that would do it. But Mum had said more than once that it wouldn't make any difference. And anyhow, I was just too scared.

*

I only had one other idea. It was a bit lame, but by that point, anything was worth a try.

I went downstairs. It was nine-thirty by now, so Mum said, 'Why're you up? Go to bed.'

'Can't sleep.'

'So eat something,' she said. Typical Mum. She's a feeder. She doesn't only feed us, she feeds all her friends that come over, Dimitri, and half the people at work. She even feeds the neighbours. Our next-door neighbours said they lost weight when we went on holiday last year because my mum wasn't taking them in food all the time.

'Not hungry,' I said.

'You need to eat,' she said raising her voice. 'You're not eating enough.' Her eyes flashed with Food Fury. That's a thing, trust me. Least, it is in Greek homes.

'There's only one thing I feel like eating,' I said.

'OK. Tell me what it is. I'll make it for you.'

'*Galaktoboureka,*' I said casually.

Mum's eyes fixed on me hard. That was Aunt Soph's speciality. Just saying its name was risky. I was worried in case she freaked out but if she did feel any emotion, she

204

didn't show it. I waited a second and added, 'Can you make me some?'

Mum barely blinked. 'Course. Not now – it's late. Tomorrow. My baby wants it, I'll make it for her.'

'I'm not a baby.'

She put her hands over both my cheeks. 'You'll always be my baby. Even when you're forty-five and you have six children.'

I rolled my eyes. 'Can you stop squashing my face? And I'm not having six children.'

She let go and said, 'I'll find a recipe.'

'Yeah, but not just any old recipe. They have to be exactly the same as . . .'

Mum stopped still and scowled at me.

'. . . as I'm used to.'

I didn't say *as Aunt Soph's* because I didn't need to. Aunt Soph made the best *galaktoboureka* in the entire universe – Mum knew it and I knew it. You'd think Mum would have had the recipe written down somewhere, but Mum made the dishes she was amazing at, and Aunt Soph made the dishes she was amazing at, and we all ate them together. That's how it always was. Who'd have guessed that one

205

day they wouldn't be talking and they'd have to make each other's?

Mum sniffed and got up. She picked up the cloth and started wiping the kitchen counter, even though it was clean. All Mum had to do was phone Aunt Soph and get the recipe. Then they'd make up and we'd go around there with pots of food and hug and cry and everything would be fine again. Uncle Dimitri and Christina would have the wedding of the century and we'd get past this and we'd make sure we never let anything come between us again. Not ever.

'I'll call Biatra,' Mum said. 'She'll have a good recipe.'

OMG. Was she never going to pick up the phone? *Call Aunt Soph*, I yelled in whale song. *Caaaalllll Aaaauuu-unnnnttt Soooooopppphhh.*

'Her mum's *galaktoboureka* are famous,' Mum continued.

Whale song wasn't working. I had to use my mouth.

'I don't want Biatra's mum's. Why don't you call—'

Mum stuck her finger in the air. 'Don't even say her name. Not happening.'

My heart plopped into my socks.

206

My lame idea hadn't worked.

So I decided to be honest. I have no idea why, after all the problems honesty's given me. 'But you're sad, Mum,' I said quietly. 'I'm worried about you.'

Mum gave me a just-about-to-cry smile. Stretchy-mouthed. Quivery-lipped. Crumple-faced. Wet-eyed.

'I'm fine, Lex,' she said. Her eyes turned gooey, like golden syrup. 'Pssshh. What a good girl I have,' she said in a voice like a rickety rope bridge. 'Heart of gold. You're an angel sent from heaven.'

And as she pulled me in for a big grabby hug, I thought, *Oh, Mum. You wouldn't say that if you knew.*

207

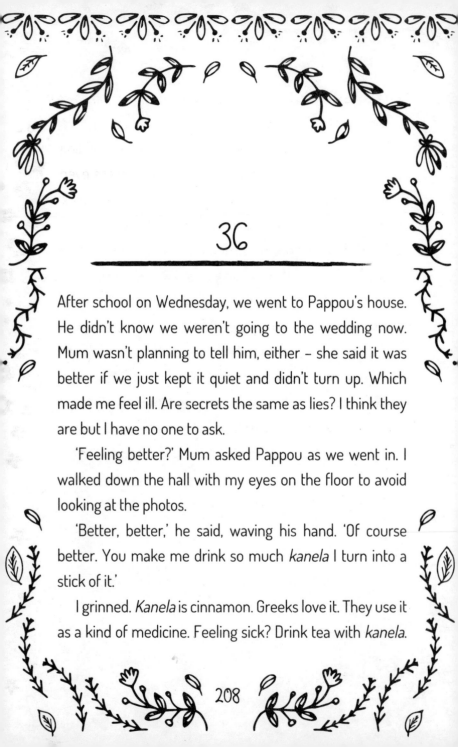

36

After school on Wednesday, we went to Pappou's house. He didn't know we weren't going to the wedding now. Mum wasn't planning to tell him, either – she said it was better if we just kept it quiet and didn't turn up. Which made me feel ill. Are secrets the same as lies? I think they are but I have no one to ask.

'Feeling better?' Mum asked Pappou as we went in. I walked down the hall with my eyes on the floor to avoid looking at the photos.

'Better, better,' he said, waving his hand. 'Of course better. You make me drink so much *kanela* I turn into a stick of it.'

I grinned. *Kanela* is cinnamon. Greeks love it. They use it as a kind of medicine. Feeling sick? Drink tea with *kanela*.

Got a cold? Tea with *kanela*. Accidently chopped your leg off with an axe? Tea with *kanela*.

'Told you,' Mum said, squeezing his tea bag and adding *kanela*. It wasn't only cinnamon, either – they were even crazier about lemon. If you were eating lamb, they ask if you wanted lemon on it. Chicken? Squeeze lemon on it. Going out? Take a wedge of lemon in case you need to squeeze it on something. I swear we'd have cereal with lemon on it if it didn't curdle the milk.

Just then, the phone rang. Pappou has a cordless phone beside him the whole time. He spends half his life on the phone. I could hear Aunt Soph's voice down the receiver from halfway across the room, and Mum must have heard it too, because she was nearer to Pappou than I was, and Aunt Soph's voice is almost as loud as my mum's.

'Sophiiiiiia,' Pappou said.

'I'm going to the shop to get more *kanela*,' Mum said to me in a low voice. Proof again that she can speak in a low voice if she really tries.

'Can I call you back a little later?' Pappou asked Aunt Soph in Greek. I'm translating in case you don't speak it. 'Evangelina is here with Lexie.'

When he said goodbye and put the phone down I said, 'How can we get them talking, Pappou?'

'I try everything,' he replied in English. I speak Greek quite well but I always answer in English, so most of the time, he speaks to me in English, or in a mixture of both that Mum calls 'Gringlish'.

He sat down on his armchair with a huffing noise and held the armrests so tightly, his knobbly knuckles went white. 'I invite them here at the same time to talk ... to talk ... but your mother, she see Sophia car outside and she drive home. Last week, I think of a new plan. I tell your mother I want her *loukomades* recipe for a neighbour.'

Loukomades are little crispy balls like doughnuts, light and airy and covered in sweet syrup. They're my mum's speciality and they're YUM.

'But really,' he went on, 'I want to give the recipe to Sophia, but to change it, make it wrong, you know? So Sophia she will make very bad *loukomades* and then she have to call your mother to ask why.'

'That's genius, Pappou!' I cried. I pulled up a chair beside his armchair, grinning even though it meant Pappou had also been lying.

210

'I know.' He winked at me. 'I'm very clever sometimes. I told your mother that everyone knows she make the best *loukomades*. You know, make her happy.'

I grinned. Yep. Mum has to make the best *loukomades* or the world will melt (or something).

'But your mother, she 'spicious. She answer me, "'Oh yeah? What's this neighbour called?"'

I laughed. Pappou did a funny impersonation of my mum, and he never managed to say words like 'suspicious' right.

'So I tell your mother, "You don't know her. Her name is Loukia Yiolides. She's Thia Niki's friend." You know what your mother told me?'

I shook my head.

'She said, "So tell this Loukia Yiolides to get a recipe from Thia Niki."'

'Your plan didn't work.'

'No. And now, I don't know what to do. Dimitri, he don't know what to do. Everybody in Greek community don't know what to do. I hope that the wedding day come and they will remember we are a family and they will stop this. They will. I'm sure. This is Dimitri wedding.' He looked at

211

me sadly, and repeated, '*Dimitri wedding*! And he marry on our wedding day – of me and Yiayia. These moment is what is important in the life. They will stop then. I know it.'

I stretched my lips out tight.

We aren't going, Pappou, I said in whale song.

But Pappou didn't speak it.

The only one I could ever wah-wah with was Eleni.

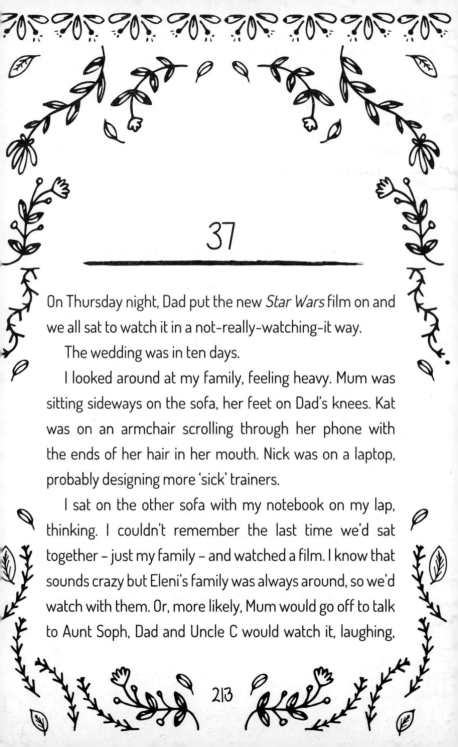

37

On Thursday night, Dad put the new *Star Wars* film on and we all sat to watch it in a not-really-watching-it way.

The wedding was in ten days.

I looked around at my family, feeling heavy. Mum was sitting sideways on the sofa, her feet on Dad's knees. Kat was on an armchair scrolling through her phone with the ends of her hair in her mouth. Nick was on a laptop, probably designing more 'sick' trainers.

I sat on the other sofa with my notebook on my lap, thinking. I couldn't remember the last time we'd sat together – just my family – and watched a film. I know that sounds crazy but Eleni's family was always around, so we'd watch with them. Or, more likely, Mum would go off to talk to Aunt Soph, Dad and Uncle C would watch it, laughing, and we'd hang with our cousins. Everything was different now. We didn't hang with them any more. But it was also kind of special for just the five of us to be in a room watching a film together. I say 'kind of' because everyone was miserable.

Name	Miserable?
Pappou	✓
Dimitri and Christina	✓
Mum and Dad	✓
Nicos	✓
Katerina	✓
Me	✓
Yiayia	✓
God	?
Eleni	?
Her family	?

When Mum went out of the room to get something, I

turned to Dad and said, 'Why don't you take her out tomorrow night? She could do with dressing up and going somewhere.'

'She never wants to. I've asked. She said she'd rather be home.'

'Take her anyway. I'll paint her nails and Kat can do her make-up – she used to love getting ready with . . .' I stopped. 'You know. Before.'

Dad said. 'What a sweetheart you are. You're such a goo—'

'Don't say "good girl",' I snapped. 'I'm really not.'

'You really are,' Dad said with a smile that made my stomach lurch.

'When you go out, can you take me to Pappou's?' I asked.

'You can stay here. Nick and Kat can babysit.'

'But I need to talk to Pappou.'

Dad scratched his big bear hairy chest, grinned, and said, 'OK. But let's see if she says yes first.'

I don't know how Dad managed it, but Mum agreed to go.

That evening, though, instead of getting ready, Mum sat

on her bed like a deflated beach ball, and said, 'I don't even feel like it.'

I stood in front of her and bit my lip. 'You're scaring me,' I said.

'Nothing to worry about. I'm just tired,' she lied in an unnaturally cheerful voice. 'Come on. Help me choose what to wear.'

I nodded, opened her wardrobe doors and pulled out some clothes. I held them in front of her and she said, 'You choose.' So I decided on a red dress with sparkles around the neck, which Mum said was a bit fancy but she didn't argue.

She had a shower, put the red dress on and we looked at the nail polishes. She picked Baby Poo Cappuccino (real name: Monte Carlo) but I told her she should have Fresh Blood Vamp Lick (real name: Candy Sweet) because it was fun and happy, and she needed fun and happy. She did a good job of acting like everything was fine, but she didn't look fine. She moved about like she had rocks inside weighing her body down.

Mum untwisted the cap and stuck out her lips. I knew she was thinking about Aunt Soph because Soph always

216

painted Mum's nails. Always. I was glad Mum missed her. Maybe she'd actually do something about it.

'I'll paint them,' I said. I slid out the small wand and the smell of the polish leaked into the air. I don't know why they all smell the same when they're different colours.

How nail polishes should smell:

Brown - hot chocolate with marshmallows
Green - freshly-mown grass
Red - strawberry jelly
Orange - mango ice cream
Blue - blueberry bubblegum
Black - Bubonic Plague

I stroked the bulging brush against the rim of the bottle and watched it ooze off like lava. Then, with a towel under her hand, which was resting on her knee, I slapped the polish on Mum's right thumb nail as badly as I could.

'Tsssch! What're you *doing*?' Mum yelled, pulling her hand back.

'I'll take the bad bits off later.'

'It's all bad bits! It's all over my finger!'

'You could pick up the phone,' I said, taking my life in my hands, 'and call Aunt Soph. She'll do your nails properly. She always has.'

To be perfectly honest (which is a stupid phrase because who in the whole world is perfectly honest?), I knew it was a stupid reason to call Aunt Soph, but I was desperate and anything was worth a try.

'KAT!' Mum yelled.

No no no! That wasn't supposed to happen!

'What?' Kat yelled from the next room.

'Come and do my nails! She's making a right pig's ear of it.'

Pig's ear? What did nails have to do with pigs' ears?

I tried not to scream. *What was going to make Mum call Aunt Soph? What?*

Kat came in, saw Mum's thumb and said, 'What, did you just lash it all over her finger? There's a nail there. Look. Nail. Finger. Not the same thing.'

Kat took off the polish and opened a bottle of base coat, which I'd fogotten about. Then she painted Mum's nails

218

neatly while I sat on Mum's bed in a mood.

Dimitri's wedding was coming, *Paska* was coming, my birthday was coming, summer was coming and we'd do all of them alone and never talk to Soph's family. I'd never see Eleni again and I'd be a lonely whale gliding through the deep blue ocean for ever.

When I returned from the ocean in my head, I realized Kat was telling Mum about something she saw on Buzz-feed and Mum was chuckling. And I wasn't sure if I'd ever seen that before. Mum always got ready with Soph while Kat and Kallie sat plotting destruction and menace somewhere else in the house.

Mum and Kat were having a moment. And that was the nicest thing I'd ever seen. Well, maybe not the nicest. But up there in the top ten. Or maybe the top fifty. Or the top five thousand. Or something.

38

Mum and Dad dropped me at Pappou's on their way out. He was watching a programme about World War II, but he turned it to a cartoon channel when I arrived without me even asking. I didn't feel like watching anything so I turned it off and we sat there in silence until he said, '*Manamu* (that means 'my love'). You visit your Pappou. You are good girl.'

I tried to smile but the little voice in my head said, *you wouldn't think that if you knew what I'd done.* I gazed at the icons. I felt so far away from the truth, and everything that was good and pure and holy. I couldn't remember the last time I'd actually been a good girl. One lie had turned into a hundred lies, and all that had happened was I didn't feel right or good or normal any more.

'You grow up and marry nice Greek boy and when you do, I give you nice present.'

'I hope it's a house or something, and not your collection of toilets,' I replied.

He laughed loudly and for ages. Once he wiped his eyes, he said, 'You want ice cream?'

I pictured the ice cream in Pappou's freezer, all yukky and old, and said, 'Umm. . . no, thanks.'

'So come look,' he said, smiling.

He shuffled into the kitchen and I followed him.

A huge new aquarium, with a clown fish and all kinds of other beautiful tropical fish I didn't know the names of, stood by the dining room wall. I loved aquariums! I'd wanted Mum to get one for ages but she said no because she'd end up cleaning the tank out.

'Pappou!' I cried. 'You got one! How come?'

'Humph,' Pappou grunted. 'Eleni-*mou*. She make me.'

'*Eleni?*'

'Of course.'

'Why? To cheer you up?'

He smiled but he didn't answer. We gazed at the fish for a while. I don't know about Pappou, but looking at them

221

definitely cheered *me* up. It was magical. It made me feel so calm and happy. I gazed at the clown fish and wished my life was as easy as his. Hers. How could you tell?

'Why can't she just phone Aunt Sophia?' I asked Pappou as I stared into the tank.

Pappou knew I wasn't talking about the clown fish. He said, 'You think she will do this?'

I turned to look at him. 'Why not?'

'Your mother she will never do this.'

'But Dimitri's wedding's coming, and then *Paska* and our birthdays and Christmas and our weddings, and—'

'You are getting married, Lexie-*mou*?'

I almost smiled. 'Not right now. But one day.'

'To a Greek boy,' he said firmly.

I rolled my eyes. 'That's not the point. They need to talk to each other.'

Pappou sighed and looked thoughtful. After a while, he said, 'Somebody have to bring the family together.' He kept his eyes on the aquarium, watching the fish. He waited for a minute and so did I because I wanted to know who that person was. It had to be Mum, right? Or did he mean Father George?

'In my head,' he continued, 'that somebody have to be you.'

'*Me?*'

My face felt hot. Did he know about the necklace?

'You.'

'I can't, Pappou. I've tried.'

'You? You are special one-in-millions blessing. You can do anything.'

I lowered my eyes. 'Eleni's the blessing. She's the miracle, not me.'

'Eleni-*mou*? Yes, she is miracle girl, but she need you.'

I blinked hard, wishing it was true. 'She doesn't need me,' I muttered. 'She's doing just fine without me.'

Pappou lifted my chin with his finger, his pale grey eyes smiling and wrinkly. He took the strand of hair hanging over my face and tucked it behind my ear. 'You listen to me,' he said. 'Long time ago, was born very special girl—'

'I know, Pappou. And her heart was bad and she nearly died, but she didn't,' I said, finishing the sentence for him.

'Yes, yes. But this is not the girl I talking about.'

I frowned but I was listening.

'This girl, when she was smaaaall, small baby, she go

223

into hospital bed of her cousin. She put her tiny hand on her cousin face and she make her feel safe. She look after her cousin then, and she look after her *always*. Imagine!' He let go of my chin and pointed his finger in the air. 'She care for her cousin all her life. She don't go play with other children because she don't want her cousin to be lonely. She make up games so her cousin she will laugh. She protect her. She love her. She put her cousin before even herself.'

Tears rolled down my cheeks and I didn't even try to hide them.

'And this girl, she not get so much attention. The light it's not shining on her. But she very special this girl.' Pappou took my hand in his huge warm paws. 'She is kind. She know what is love and what is family.'

I bit my lip to stop it from wobbling but it didn't work. Pappou smiled at me and for a split second, I wondered if he knew what I'd done. But he couldn't have. He couldn't have spent six months suffering like this just to see if I'd own up.

'This girl,' he continued, 'she the strong one. Not Eleni-*mou*.'

I shook my head. I didn't feel strong.

'Why you say no? Is true. Eleni-*mou*, she . . . need . . . you. She stay here in the world because of you. She make me get this fishes because of you.' He let go of my hand and waved at the aquarium.

'Because of *me*?'

'Course because of you. She tell me you sad. She want make you happy so she tell me buy fishes. See? She love you. But she cannot fix this. I cannot fix this. Even Yiayia,' he said, pointing up, 'she cannot fix this. Maybe you, Lexie-*mou*.'

'But, Pappou,' I croaked. 'I don't know how to.'

'You?' he roared. 'With love so big in your heart? God send you to our family. You angel from . . .' and he pointed up.

And I thought, *Oh Pappou. How am I ever going to tell you?*

39

I went upstairs and locked myself in the bathroom with my notebook.

I had to think. Pappou was right. Not that I'd been sent by God or the angels, but that my family meant everything to me. It meant everything to all of us.

I picked up my pen and started writing.

Our families need each other in a million huge, tiny and crazy ways. When I hid the necklace and told the lie, it wasn't because I didn't care. It was because I did.

- I cared about my mum and how hurt she would be.
- I cared about Anastasia coming between Eleni and me.
- And I cared that the necklace wouldn't be handed down to who it was meant to be handed down to, and it would interfere with the cosmic order of the world (or something).

But all I've done is mess everything up.

I cried into the shower curtain for a while. For the record, shower curtains are not good to cry into. I had no idea how to make it better. I needed help. Preferably from God, but I'd already asked him and he hadn't answered.

Maybe, I thought, wiping my nose on a tissue instead (which, for the record, is much more absorbent – but you probably knew that), *maybe I was asking the wrong person.*

I crept out of the bathroom and slipped into Pappou and Yiayia's room. The clock on the wall was ticking and a

227

car alarm went off outside, which made me nervous, like time was running out and an emergency was happening at the same time.

I needed to talk to Yiayia. She wasn't there, obviously, even though it felt like she was, so I quietly opened the wardrobe door and stood for a moment, looking at her clothes. After a while, I picked up one of her cardigans and held it to my nose. Yiayia's goodness and loveliness flooded over me and I felt ashamed.

I remembered how it was when she was alive, how warm and close and happy we all were. And I remembered her. How her face creased into a hundred ridges when she smiled and the skin on her hands was as thin as paper. I remembered her laugh, and the way she danced at parties, and how she never said a bad word about anyone. She'd taught us to be kind and honest and good. And I'd failed her.

I whispered, 'Yiayia, I'm sorry. Please help me. Tell me what to do.'

I knew her answer would be, 'Tellllll theeeemmm yoooou haaaave the neeeeccccclaaaaaace'.

So I whispered, 'Anything but that. They'll be angrier

than the angriest they've ever been. Ever. Ever. Ever.'

Yiayia said, 'Therrrreee issss no oooootherrrrr solllutiooooon.'

'They wiiiilll kiiillll meeeeee,' I replied. 'And ittttt woooonnnnn't heeeellllpppppp annnyywaaayyyy.'

'*Doooo iiiitttttt*,' she said.

I sighed and stared at the ceiling for ages.

'*Ooookkkkkkk, I wiiiilllllll*,' I said, eventually. '*I'll doooo iiittttttt*.'

I kissed her cardigan, put it back and closed the wardrobe doors.

She was right.

I had to do it. And I had to do it now.

I went downstairs to tell Pappou everything, but half-way down, I could hear him on the phone, talking in Greek.

As soon as I walked in the room, I knew something was wrong.

'Oy oy oy. And what did the doctors say? Tssshhh. Tsssh.' He looked at me and his eyes told me everything. 'They're going to operate? When? We'll come right now.'

I froze. 'Pappou?'

He said, 'It's Eleni-*mou*.'

229

40

I dropped to my knees. I'd never lost the ability to stand up before but it's actually a thing. Your legs give way like thin table legs that snap, and down you go.

Pappou picked me up and sat me on his armchair. I crawled into a ball and stayed like that.

I was sure that if something happened to her, I'd know. How did I not feel it?

I couldn't tell Pappou about the necklace now, not when we had an Eleni emergency to deal with. He phoned my parents and they left the restaurant immediately. Pappou sat beside me, rubbing my back, but I didn't move – I just lay there, stiff and tense. It took a thousand hundred years for my parents' car to pull up in the drive.

Dad rushed in, picked me up and held me tight in his big

bear arms. I only started crying then. He stroked my head and said in my ear, 'I'll take you to her right now, OK?' He turned to Pappou. 'Is she at Croydon U?' Croydon University Hospital was where Eleni and I were born. It has a cardiology unit, where Eleni had her operations and I was placed inside her cot. Pappou nodded, so Dad said, 'Let's go.'

Mum was standing in the hallway like a ghost.

'My glasses, Evangelina,' Pappou said in Greek. 'My glasses. I don't know where they are.'

Mum woke up then and went searching as Dad opened the front door.

'Dad,' I breathed in his ear. 'What if she's—'

'Don't even think it,' Dad replied. 'She's going to make it. I'll drive you guys there and go home for Kat and Nick.'

Mum found the glasses in the kitchen and held them out to Pappou, who was putting on his coat. He looked old and shaky and not ready for another tragedy, not that anyone ever is. Dad put me down, held my coat out so I could put my arms inside, and led me by the hand to the car. All the noises seemed so loud. The gravel under our feet. The front door closing. The car being unlocked by the

231

remote control. The doors slamming shut. The engine revving.

We drove to the hospital, and all the way, nobody said a single word.

The lights in the lobby were bright and the hospital smelt serious and medical. It was busy in there. Most of the chairs were full. Nurses strode past. A woman with grey hair limped by on crutches and a man sat near us with a bandage around his head. Mum's red dress was too fancy for the hospital, and Pappou's hands were shaking.

We hurried past reception to the cardiology department. When we reached the Heart Centre, Dad took my hand and asked a nurse where Eleni was. She told us the room number, and we were hurrying towards it when we saw Kallie and Elias sitting in the corridor outside the room. They stood up when they saw us, their eyes shiny with shock.

'Guys,' Dad said warmly. 'How is she?'

'We don't know yet,' Elias replied in a husky voice. 'Hi, Pappou.' He gave Pappou a hug and so did Kallie. It was awkward for a second because no one knew what to do.

But then Dad let go of my hand, stepped towards Elias, stretched his arms out and enveloped him. 'Ffffffffffffff,' he said, mid-hug. 'Missed you guys so much. So much.'

'Us too,' Elias murmured.

Mum smiled weakly at Kallie, gave her a stiff, clumsy hug and said, 'Where's your mum?'

'In there.' Kallie pointed to the door. 'With Dad. Eleni . . . she collapsed in the kitchen. We don't know if . . . we don't know anything yet. Except . . . we know it's bad. Are Kat and Nick here?' she asked, looking down the corridor.

'Not yet. I'm going to get them,' Dad said. 'In fact, can you call them, Kal? Tell them to get a cab? I'll pay when it gets here.'

'Sure. Elias, come out with me. There's no reception in here.' Elias nodded and followed Kallie down the corridor.

I sat on a chair and Pappou sat next to me. On the wall were paintings done by local children called Amar and Nadine. Above were bright strip lights, and signs directing people to other wards. Below were shiny squeaky green floors. And behind the door of Room 8, Eleni lay in a bed, strapped to machines. Maybe dying. Maybe even—

The door opened and Uncle C came out. When he saw

233

my Dad, they didn't say a word, they just walked towards each other, wrapped their arms around each other and stayed there for ages. When they let go, Uncle C's eyes were red and wet. And I thought, *That's it. We're too late.*

'She's hanging on in there,' Uncle Christos said, wiping his eyes with the palm of his hand. 'Just about. Doctors are doing more tests.' He turned to me and said, 'After she collapsed, when she was still with it, she asked for you, Lexie-*mou.*'

My insides squeezed together but I couldn't speak.

I wasn't there for her.

She'd collapsed and asked for me and I hadn't even heard her whale song.

Uncle C put his arms around my mum and said, 'Soph'll be happy you came, Ange.'

I heard Mum whisper, 'Course. She's my sister.'

234

41

Uncle C asked us to look out for his parents, who were on their way, and he went back into the room. Mum kept her eyes glued to the floor. Dad was grinding his hands together and Pappou was staring ahead, looking old and tired.

When the door opened again, Uncle C came out with Aunt Soph behind him. She closed the door so I couldn't see in, but I could hear machines beeping. Aunt Soph's cheeks were smeared with make-up. She looked worn out, like she'd just run a hundred miles without stopping and her body was about to crumple to the floor.

Mum saw her and her hand shot to cover her mouth.

In a split second, my dad's huge arms reached around Mum and Soph and pulled them together. Mum's arms slid around Soph's shoulders and Soph started sobbing so hard her body was juddering. Uncle Christos put his arms around them too, and the four of them stood there like that for over a minute.

I glanced at Pappou. He was looking upwards and mouthing something under his breath. I couldn't hear what it was, but I think he was thanking God. Or Yiayia. Or maybe the ceiling.

'How is she?' Mum asked when Dad let go of everyone and they stood wiping their noses.

Aunt Soph replied, 'She's not conscious. They're deciding whether to operate.'

She came over to where I was sitting, held the tops of my arms and looked at me with such despair in her eyes, it made my guts shrivel. 'She missed you so much, Lex,' she murmured. Then she moved over to Pappou and squatted beside him, holding his hand.

I stared at my Kickers as they knocked together with a *tap-tap-tap*.

Stay with me, Eleni, I called in whale song. *Please. I'm sorry I lied about Yiayia and the necklace.*

Just then, the door opened and the doctors called Aunt Soph and Uncle Christos back into the room. A black nurse with red glasses came over from the reception bay and told us we could wait in the waiting room. 'Might be a while,' she

236

said kindly. 'Especially if they're going to operate. There's a coffee machine in there and it's quiet. Maybe you should take your children home?' she suggested to Mum and Dad. 'It could be a long night.'

'They're staying right here with us,' my dad said, taking my hand and smiling at her.

'Inseparable family, eh?' she said, beaming. 'Good. That's what it's all about.'

And I thought, *Inseparable family?*

Hah!

Don't get me started.

Ten minutes later, Aunt Soph and Uncle C came out looking pale. A nurse gave them some forms to sign, which must have been hard because Aunt Soph started shaking her head. She was so upset, I had to turn my eyes away and look somewhere else.

Once they'd signed them, Aunt Soph came over to me and said in a shaky voice, 'Lex. They don't know if she'll . . . if she's going to make it.' Her face creased and she whispered, 'Will you come?'

I nodded, and Aunt Soph led me by the hand into the room.

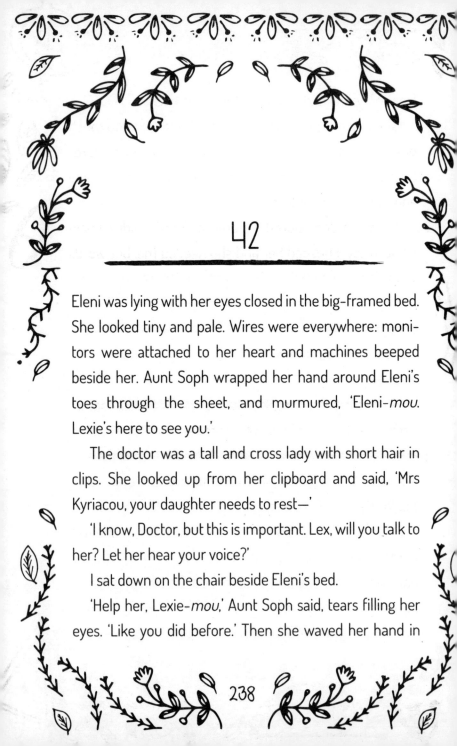

42

Eleni was lying with her eyes closed in the big-framed bed. She looked tiny and pale. Wires were everywhere: monitors were attached to her heart and machines beeped beside her. Aunt Soph wrapped her hand around Eleni's toes through the sheet, and murmured, 'Eleni-*mou*. Lexie's here to see you.'

The doctor was a tall and cross lady with short hair in clips. She looked up from her clipboard and said, 'Mrs Kyriacou, your daughter needs to rest—'

'I know, Doctor, but this is important. Lex, will you talk to her? Let her hear your voice?'

I sat down on the chair beside Eleni's bed.

'Help her, Lexie-*mou*,' Aunt Soph said, tears filling her eyes. 'Like you did before.' Then she waved her hand in

front of her face to show she couldn't talk, and went out.

The doctor said, 'Fine, but be very careful not to touch or pull anything off Eleni. Just let her know you're here.' She checked a machine and then went out, leaving Eleni and me in the room alone.

Once the door closed, I stared at Eleni. I didn't know what to say. I needed her and she needed me, but words weren't going to help. Not now. In the background, the machine strapped to Eleni's heart went beep . . . beep . . . beep.

I thought of reaching out and holding her hand but it wasn't enough.

So, without thinking, I stood up and pulled the covers back very slowly, being careful of all the wires. I sat on the bed, then lay down carefully, and moved my body over in millimetres until it was next to hers. Then I made sure her blanket was covering her so she wouldn't get cold. I couldn't put my hand on top of her scar because she had monitors on her heart, so I took her cool, limp hand in mine and rested my head on her shoulder. Very gently, I squeezed her hand, and whispered, 'I'm here, Eleni-*mou*. And I'm not going ever again.'

I felt her lungs breathe a big juddery breath, like she was sighing with relief.

I lay with her in the silence, talking to her in whale song. I wasn't sure if it worked any more but I tried anyway. I heard footsteps outside the door, and added quietly, in actual words, 'Your doctor's frowny and mean. I'm definitely not her. You can be her. I'm Christina.'

The door opened and the frowny doctor came back in. She gasped, rushed to Eleni's bedside with wild eyes, and hissed at me to get out.

'I've only been here ten seconds,' I lied.

'You shouldn't be in there at all!' she snapped. 'Your cousin's very sick.'

'She's not my cousin,' I replied from beside Eleni. 'She's my twin.'

Before the doctor could argue, Aunt Soph came in. She saw me inching out of Eleni's bed, and instead of being angry, she nodded at me, smiled the saddest smile in the whole world, and mouthed, *Thank you.*

When I went back into the waiting room, it was 11.30 p.m. but time didn't seem real. The clock was just a white circle

240

of plastic with black hands going around very, very slowly. Kat and Nick were sitting on the floor, with Nicos next to Elias, and Kallie on the other side of Kat with her head on her shoulder. Uncle C's parents had arrived along with his brother Pani, and so had Uncle Dimitri and Christina. According to Christina, half of the Greek population of London had gathered in our church to light candles and pray for Eleni.

The nurse brought Pappou a soft armchair so he'd be comfortable, but he still looked crooked and crumpled. Mum made me a bed by pushing two soft chairs together but I couldn't sleep. How could I? All I could think of was Eleni. Aunt Soph and Uncle C stayed in the room with her but there wasn't much space in there for me too, and the doctor was angry with me anyway.

At around four a.m., I went to the toilet, and when I came back, I stood outside the waiting room door. Through the glass, I could see Dad's arm around Mum, Kat and Nick sitting with Kallie and Elias, and Pappou talking to Uncle C's parents, his eyes bleary and his hands around a paper cup of coffee. The room was full of people, all brought together again, and that was just a tiny fraction of our family and

friends who were by their phones, on standby, waiting for news.

We stayed in the waiting room until morning.

Eleni made it through the night.

The next day, the angry doctor stopped being angry, and let me lie next to Eleni again.

Eleni made it through that day, too.

And the night after that.

And the next day.

She wasn't OK, not by a long shot.

But six days later, she was allowed out of hospital for Uncle Dimitri's wedding.

43

The hotel where they were having it was super fancy.

Our family stood in the reception room together, wearing glittery dresses, pinchy shiny shoes and smart suits. Mum and Aunt Soph, their nails perfectly painted and their arms linked, stood beside each other, and next to Aunt Soph was Eleni, grinning at me like a smiley-face emoji.

She was in a wheelchair and she was pale. She had an oxygen machine beside her, a tube going into her nose and a nurse pushing her chair. The situation was bad: Eleni needed a new heart. I would have offered her mine but I knew our families would freak out at that idea because I kind of needed it myself. Eleni was on a transplant list, and as bad as that was, it wasn't the worst part.

The worst part was that someone else had to die in order for her to stay alive. Someone our age and our size. And that was more awful than any of us could bear to think about.

So we distracted ourselves. It was Uncle Dimitri and Christina's wedding, after all.

Christina looked like a movie star. She had a long, cream, lace wedding dress, and her hair was half up and decorated with white flowers.

'I'm her,' Eleni said, gazing at her.

'Uh-uh. I'm her. You can be her.' I pointed to Christina's great-grandma, who was about a hundred and ninety and was wearing a gold flowery dress.

Eleni giggled. '*You're* her.'

'*You* are.'

It went on for a while. I won't bore you.

There were lots of nail polish colours on the guests' nails, so we named them, and I wrote them down in my notebook. Which I took to the wedding. Which Mum wasn't happy about.

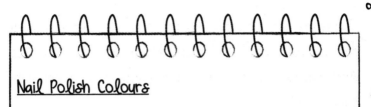

Nail Polish Colours

- Sunset Over Goldfish Mountain.
- Sugar Addict's Dental Fillings.
- Very Smelly Cherry Jelly.
- Dragon on Fire in a Far-Away Land.
- Puke of a Screaming Leprechaun (Kallie's).

It was fun.

No one really watches you at weddings, so you can get up to all kinds of stuff. Nicos and Elias were having a who-can-eat-the-most-*meze* competition, and Kat and Kallie were making some younger cousins get them drinks, like they were their slaves. Eleni, in the wheelchair next to me, was counting things. Don't ask me what.

After the meal, Mum, in a blue dress and silver heels, her hair falling down her back in loose curls, danced with Pappou, who was in a smart suit. Dad, all in white because he thought he looked stylish (wrong), sat with Uncle C,

talking and laughing.

Eleni and I were alone at the table. Well, her nurse was there, but she was busy eating and saying how delicious everything was.

It was time to have *that conversation* with Eleni. So I took her hand and said, 'I'm sorry. That I lied.'

Eleni tried to wrinkle her nose but the breathing tube was in the way. 'I shouldn't have told you to,' she said. 'But I never thought you really *would*.'

I smiled but my stomach was churning.

'Forget it,' Eleni said. 'It's OK. We're all talking again, and that's what matters.'

'It's not OK,' I mumbled. 'I need to make it right. I need to tell them the truth.'

'The necklace has disappeared anyway,' Eleni said, 'which is a shame because it would have looked soooo pretty on Christina.'

I bit my lip.

She didn't get to wear it and it was all my fault.

After a crazy hour of the adults holding hands and dancing in circles to the Greek band, and pinning thousands of hundreds of pounds (as Eleni called it) on Uncle Dimitri and Christina, it was time for the speeches.

As my dad made a whole series of cheesy dad jokes in his *kumberos* speech, I gazed at the ceiling and took a deep breath. When he finished, I walked over to the bride and groom's table, whispered in the middle of Uncle Dimitri and Christina's heads so they could both hear, and they nodded.

Dimitri called over his friend, George, who was doing the introductions, and he went on stage and said, 'Ladies and gentlemen, can I have your attention, please? We have one more speaker this evening. A big round of applause for . . . Lexie Efthimiou!'

A ripple of applause went around the room. The spotlight landed on me and I walked slowly up to the stage. My feet felt heavy as space boots on the moon, and I lifted and put them down like I was figuring out gravity. Panic gripped me and I felt the urge to turn and run, but I carried on going.

Spotlights are roasting hot. How do singers do it?

Faces in the darkness turned my way as I stood in front of the microphone. It looked like a dark ocean full of hungry sharks.

'Um . . .' I began. The microphone whistled loudly, deafening everyone. George ran over and tapped it a couple of times, which did precisely nothing, but I think it made him happy.

'I'm Lexie. Dimitri's niece,' I said in a croaky voice. I chewed the inside of my lip as they clapped again. I don't know why they were clapping because I hadn't really said anything yet.

'I . . . er . . . well, I have something important to say.'

Mum was looking at me in shock. I'd never got up in front of everyone willingly in my life and she couldn't work out what I was doing. I looked over at Eleni in her wheelchair and even though I couldn't see her face in the darkness, I knew she was grinning at me.

I took the deepest breath I could take without my lungs exploding and said, 'I know I should be up here talking about Uncle Dimitri and his amazing girlfriend, Christina—'

'WIFE!' everyone yelled.

'Wife! Sorry! *Wife*. But that's not what I want to say. This is a happy night, but the last few months haven't been happy at all, and—'

248

'Lexie-*mou*,' Dad boomed, his voice so loud he didn't need a microphone. 'This is not the time—'

'Dad, this *is* the time,' I said. 'I have something to say.'

The wedding hall fell silent.

'Our family has just been through the most difficult year of our lives, which I'm sure everyone here knows about. Our Yiayia died and my family didn't talk to Eleni's family for six months.'

Somebody shouted something but I didn't hear what it was, so I carried on going.

'I told a lie, and now it's time to tell the truth.'

The spotlights burnt into my skin. Someone turned the main lights up a little so I could see their faces, and shushed loudly so the whole room went quiet. I blinked hard and looked at my mother with tears in my eyes. My hands were clammy and hot and I wiped them on my dress.

'Mum,' I began, 'I'm sorry to tell you this in front of everyone, but...' I took a breath and swallowed. 'Yiayia did want Eleni to have the necklace.'

My mother stared at me and put her fingers over her mouth.

249

'She . . . she told us the night of the engagement party. She promised it to Eleni. Not because she didn't want you to have it, but because she made a deal with Eleni so she'd stay alive.'

Tears stung my eyes and my throat blocked up because it was so hard to tell my mum the truth. I knew how much it was going to hurt her. There was a rumbling of talking now but Mum was still glaring at me, so I added, 'I'm so sorry I lied to you.'

Dad stood up. 'Lexie, come down,' he said. 'You don't need to do this.'

'I do,' I said, trying not to cry. 'Because there's something else I need to tell you.'

I waited until the whole place was silent. And then I dropped the bomb.

'I was the one who took Yiayia's necklace.'

Well.

That made the roof blast off.

44

I couldn't carry on after that because everyone yelled and jumped up and ran to me and started asking a million questions (I felt bad for Dimitri and Christina, but they kind of liked the drama of it, I could tell).

No one could believe it.

I explained to my parents and Pappou how I hated seeing my mum and Aunt Soph fighting, and I thought that if there was no necklace, it would all blow over and we'd go back to how we were before.

'I'm so sorry,' I said, waiting for the biggest telling-off ever, and a punishment that lasted until I was eighty-two years old. If I was lucky.

But for some crazy reason, my mum and Aunt Soph started laughing. I was trying to work out why when Kat and Nick came over.

'Siiick one, sis,' Nicos said, and gave me a high five.

'Oh my God! I can't believe it!' Kat shrieked. 'Who'd have thought my goodie-goodie little sister would lie and steal and—'

'Yeah, all right, Kat,' I muttered.

'Look, you tried to stop them arguing. You did what you thought was right. I have massive respect for that, even though you messed up on a truly epic scale. Honestly, Lex. When you got up on that stage and told the whole wedding you took the necklace, you know what I thought?'

I shook my head. I wasn't sure I wanted to know.

'I thought, *I'm her.*'

And Eleni, in her wheelchair beside me, laughed her head off.

Kat always hated us playing that game.

Two days after the wedding, we went to Pappou's house and sat around the table.

Again.

I felt like an important business person having

252

meetings all the time, but also like a criminal being interviewed again and again by the police.

My family was there, and Eleni's, too. Uncle Dimitri and Christina were on their honeymoon by then, but some of my parents' cousins from Cyprus were still around, and there were one or two of those old, wrinkly family friends who always ask, 'Do you know who I am?' with a big smile, and you nod because you don't want to be rude but you actually have no clue.

It was the first time our two families had been at Pappou's house together since the argument about the necklace. Eleni was allowed out of hospital again, but just for the day. Uncle C pushed her wheelchair towards me and she took my hand.

'Thanks for the aquarium,' I said. 'And the clown fish. I love them. And thanks for telling Kyria Maria about the window.'

Eleni shook her head. 'That wasn't me. It was Anastasia.'

'*What?*'

'She phoned Kyria Maria herself to tell her what happened. She doesn't expect you to be her friend or anything, but she told me to tell you she's sorry she didn't stick up for you. Demi's mum paid for the window.'

253

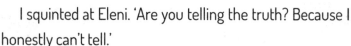

I squinted at Eleni. 'Are you telling the truth? Because I honestly can't tell.'

'Yeah,' Eleni chuckled. 'Anastasia knows she wasn't very nice to you. She said she was angry about moving and leaving her friends behind, and seeing the two of us together made her want to be mean. I told her off and said that's not the best way to make new friends. She is really nice, though, Lex. Honest.'

I thought about that for a minute. 'If she's sorry, she needs to say it to me,' I said. 'But I guess I need to say it to her as well. It's hard being separated from your friends. I didn't think about that before, but I totally get it now.'

'OK, everybody!' Pappou yelled. (He pronounces it 'ev-irry-buddy'.) 'Please be quiet.'

Everyone went quiet. Kind of. Our families were pretty chatty since we'd started hanging out again – we had six months of stuff to catch up on, after all.

Pappou sat down, put his hand into a black velvet bag and took out a small green box. Then he lifted the lid and the room went quiet as he pulled out the wedding necklace.

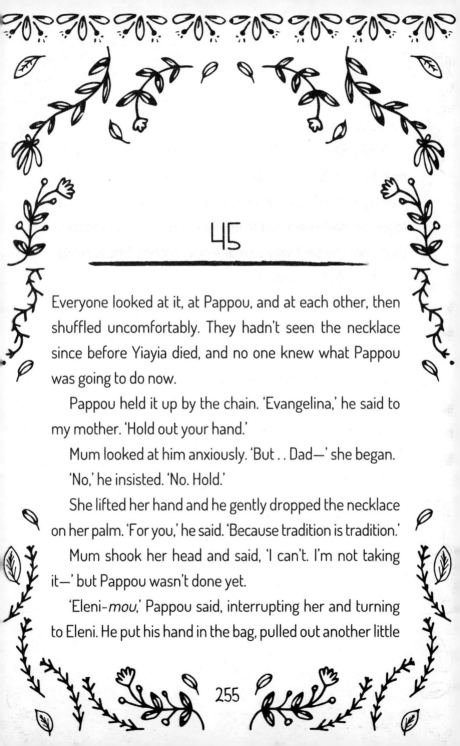

45

Everyone looked at it, at Pappou, and at each other, then shuffled uncomfortably. They hadn't seen the necklace since before Yiayia died, and no one knew what Pappou was going to do now.

Pappou held it up by the chain. 'Evangelina,' he said to my mother. 'Hold out your hand.'

Mum looked at him anxiously. 'But . . Dad—' she began.

'No,' he insisted. 'No. Hold.'

She lifted her hand and he gently dropped the necklace on her palm. 'For you,' he said. 'Because tradition is tradition.'

Mum shook her head and said, 'I can't. I'm not taking it—' but Pappou wasn't done yet.

'Eleni-*mou*,' Pappou said, interrupting her and turning to Eleni. He put his hand in the bag, pulled out another little box and said, 'Little Eleni-*mou*. Hold out your hand.'

Mum went quiet and frowned. Eleni leant forward in her wheelchair and held her hand out. Pappou opened the lid of the box and lifted out another necklace, identical to the first. Everyone in the room gasped.

Pappou dropped it into Eleni's palm.

'For you. Because a promise is a promise,' he said. And then he winked at her. Everyone in the room was so shocked.

Everyone except me.

Because when I gave Yiayia's wedding necklace back to Pappou, I had a little chat with him and told him my idea. I suggested making another necklace, the same as the original, so that Mum and Eleni would both be happy. And that way, our family traditions would carry on, but Yiayia's promise and her deal with God would be kept, too.

Pappou had given me a huge hug and told me that his granddaughter was the cleverest girl in the whole world. Which isn't true, but that's OK. I'm not so bothered by lies any more.

The way I see it is this. Truth isn't one single perfect thing. What's true for you probably isn't the same as what's true for me. And what's true today might not be true in a

week or a year or even this evening. Truth can change, and that makes it tricky. I still don't know when I should be honest and when I should lie because telling the truth might make God love you but it doesn't make everyone else love you. People don't race to your side and high-five you for your sparkling honesty, whatever adults might tell you. And I have no idea why parents say you should always tell the truth and then make up all kinds of stuff themselves.

But I think it's OK to tell a small lie if it makes someone feel happy.

You can say your brother's new trainers are *siiiick* when they really just look like vomit.

And it's OK to lie to stop someone getting in trouble and making everyone hate you. You can say you have no idea who did it but the keys are in the sea, so someone needs to wade in and get them out. But the lies that hurt – the ones that split families up – those are the ones you should avoid. Not that I know what they are. I don't know if I'll ever work it out.

Anyhow.

Pappou winked at me and I winked back. We'd done it. We'd fixed the problem. And it felt great.

But Pappou wasn't finished.

He put his hand in the bag and pulled out another small box.

'Lexie-*mou*,' he said, looking at me with his eyes so full of love, it made my insides squeeze together. 'Hold out your hand.'

I frowned but he nodded and said, 'Hold.'

I searched his face, trying to work out what he was doing, and slowly held up my palm. Pappou opened the lid of the box. He held up a third necklace, and said, 'For you. For being brave girl and telling the truth.'

'But—' I began, my eyes scanning the sea of bewildered faces in front of me. I really didn't deserve it, not after what I did.

'No but but. For you. For take care of Eleni all this years, and try to make our family come together again. You did a bad thing. And then you did a good thing. A very very good thing.'

'But . . . Dad,' my mum asked, looking carefully at all three necklaces, 'which one's the original?

'Hah!' Pappou roared. 'I tell you truth. I don't even know myself.' And he winked at me again.

Huh. So much for honesty.

258

I looked down at my necklace. And then I started chuckling. Because there were lots of versions of the necklace now, just like there were lots of versions of the truth. And that made sense. Least, it did to me.

'And now,' Aunt Sophia yelled, 'it's time to eat!'

We took our seats around the table, buzzing and talking and laughing, and out came plates and plates of food.

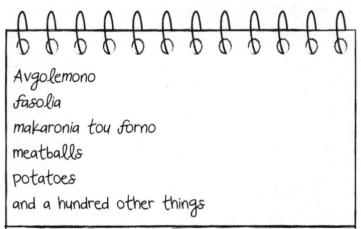

Avgolemono
fasolia
makaronia tou forno
meatballs
potatoes
and a hundred other things

We ate until we were bursting at the seams.

And Yiayia, up in the Greek part of heaven, was smiling and smiling and smiling.

The End

Loukia's Cinnamon Cake

Yiayia's cinnamon cake recipe is the one her friend, Loukia Yiolides (who owned a bakery) used to make. This is the recipe. Most Greek recipes are REALLY COMPLICATED but this is easy to make, even for me. Make sure you get a grown-up to help, especially with the oven, the hob and cutting the cake.

Makes 1 traybake/20 generous pieces

Ingredients
400g self-raising flour
180g caster sugar
Pinch of salt
2 teaspoons baking powder
2 eggs
275ml milk
2 teaspoons vanilla extract
100g butter, melted

For the marbling
250g softened butter
100g soft brown sugar
2 tablespoons plain flour
2 teaspoons ground cinnamon

For the glaze
175g icing sugar, sifted
3½ tablespoons of milk
1 teaspoon vanilla extract

1. Preheat the oven to 180°C/gas mark 4 and grease and line a baking dish, about 25 x 30cm.

2. For the marbling, beat the softened butter in a bowl until very soft (almost runny); unless your kitchen is very warm you may need to place the bowl briefly over a pan of hot water to loosen the butter. Beat in the sugar, flour and cinnamon until smooth, then set aside.

3. For the cake batter, mix the flour, sugar, salt and baking powder together in a bowl. Using electric beaters, beat the eggs, milk and vanilla extract into the dry ingredients until smooth. Add the melted butter gradually, still using the electric beaters, until you have a smooth, very thick batter. Transfer the mixture to the lined baking dish and spread it out gently to the edges of the dish.

4. Spoon the marbling mixture evenly over the top of the batter and, using a fork, swirl the marbling through the mixture to create a marbled, streaky effect; don't overwork it, as you don't want the marbling to blend with the batter.

5. Transfer the dish to a middle shelf in the oven and bake for 50–60 minutes, until a skewer inserted into the middle comes out clean. If it starts to brown too much before the middle is set, cover loosely with foil.

6. Mix the glaze ingredients together in a jug and, while the cake is still warm, pour evenly over the top, waiting for each addition to be absorbed before pouring over more. Leave to cool and set a little before cutting into pieces to serve, ideally while still warm.

Theo Michaels's Galaktoboureka

Aunt Soph's galaktoboureka recipe is a closely guarded secret, so I asked my cousin, Theo Michaels, for one instead. He was on UK MasterChef and is now a well-known chef with his own cookbooks and everything, so if you ask me he's definitely a top-ranking cousin. Don't forget to ask a grown-up for help with the oven, the hob and the knife.

Ingredients
140g butter, melted
1 pack (about 250g) filo pastry (or 12 sheets)

For the custard
1 litre whole milk
100g caster sugar
100g cornflour
3 egg yolks, lightly beaten
1 vanilla pod, split lengthways and seeds scraped out

For the syrup
350g caster sugar
350ml water
Small squeeze of lemon juice
5 cloves

1. To make the custard, put the milk, sugar, cornflour and egg yolks into a pan. Add the vanilla seeds (save the pod to put in your sugar jar) and bring to a gentle simmer, stirring constantly and making sure the mixture doesn't boil (or the eggs will scramble). Once thickened, remove from the heat and set aside to cool a little and firm up more. Preheat the oven to 180°C/gas mark 4.

2. For the syrup, put the sugar, water, lemon juice and cloves into a pan, stir to mix then gently heat until the sugar has dissolved. Increase the heat and simmer for 5 minutes, until very slightly thickened, then remove from the heat and set aside to cool completely. Remove the cloves with a spoon.

3. Brush the base and sides of a baking tin, about 24 x 28cm, with plenty of melted butter, then line the base with a sheet of filo. Brush the pastry generously with melted butter and layer over another 5 sheets of filo, brushing with plenty of melted butter between each layer.

4. Pour the thickened custard over the top of the filo and spread it out gently in an even layer; it should be about 2.5cm deep. Top the custard with another sheet of filo, brushing generously with butter as with the base, and continue with a further 5 sheets of filo, brushing each with butter. You are in essence making a custard and filo pastry sandwich!

5. If there is any excess filo around the edges, fold it back in towards the middle and give a final brush of melted butter over the top. Using the tip of a sharp knife, score a diamond pattern into the top layer of filo. Splash some water over the pastry (wetting your hand and shaking it over the top) and bake in the oven for 40—45 minutes, or until golden brown. If the pastry starts to turn too dark, cover loosely with foil (you want the bottom layers of filo to crisp up, and this takes longer than the top).

6. Remove from the oven and let it sit for 15 minutes, then pour over the sugar syrup and leave for about an hour to let it soak in.

7. Cut into pieces along the scored lines and devour!

www.TheoMichaels.com

Acknowledgements

Writing about a Greek Cypriot family in Britain was tricky because it was a world I knew nothing about. I contacted Alexandra Strick of Inclusive Minds, whose ambassador programme puts authors in touch with young people from a wide range of cultures to support and encourage diversity in children's books. I have Alex to thank for introducing me to Biatra Christou, who invited me to East Croydon to meet her, Aredi and Loukia. I later met Loukia's brother Andreas and her parents, George and Sonia Giorgiou, who told me about Greek Cypriot family life and their community. Huge thanks to you all, especially Loukia Yiolides, who's answered a 'thousand hundred' texts and emails over the last year and doesn't mind that I've included her family's lace tablecloths, numerous freezers and garden-toilet decorations in this book. Thanks to Fiona Dunbar for putting me in touch with Mary Tryfonos, who read a draft of *Lexie* and gave feedback. Thanks also to librarian Tanya Efthimiou, champion of children's books, and her wonderful daughter Alex, who read and offered excellent advice. Alex described life as a Greek Cypriot teenager and corrected my Greek grammar: in your honour, Alex, I've given Lexie your name.

The week before Christmas, just as the book was going to print, I read about Greek Cypriot UK *Masterchef* contestant Theo Michaels in a food magazine, and quickly contacted him to ask if he'd be willing to send me a recipe for *galaktoboureka* and he agreed! What a dude! That's a top chef's recipe, people. Enjoy.

My agent, Hilary Delamere, is brilliant: I have everything to thank her for, as well as Barry, Rachel H, Elinor, Laura and the Chicken House team – there would be no book without you. Reverence and homage to Editor of the Year (to my mind), Rachel Leyshon, who, with characteristic sensitivity and insight, turned a rambling mess of words and ideas into a story, and who told me about sisters she once knew who argued over a family heirloom and never spoke again.

My daughter Maayan deserves huge kudos, too. Sadly, she doesn't read but she watches lots of movies and TV programmes, which have clearly taught her much about storytelling and drama because when I was utterly stuck, she sat cross-legged beside me on the sofa and said,

'Mum, this is what needs to happen.' Her previous plot suggestion was to kill everyone, so I wasn't keen on asking her again, but this time, she told me Lexie needed to climb into Eleni's hospital bed beside her, and she was right. Thanks, Mymy.

Lastly – mostly – thanks to my family: my other children, Tamar (guardian of bones and tissues), Maor (guardian of our land) and Natan (guardian of life hacks); my mother (of course); my sisters; my cousins (disclaimer: I don't *really* have a list of cousin rankings) and my friends, in the UK and across the world, for keeping me smiling, helping me in countless ways, and enriching my life. I love you all big time, and I'm not even lying. Honest.